I0583871

DOWNWIND, ALICE

by C.C. Adams

DOWNWIND, ALICE

by C.C. Adams

Lycan Valley Press Publications
1625 E 72nd St STE 700 PMB 132
Tacoma, Washington 98404 United States of America

Printed in the United States of America

First Edition, October 2020

ISBN-13: 978-1-64562-969-6

Cover by Greg Chapman © 2020 DAP Publications

© Copyright Alice Conway etc. 2020 C.C. Adams

This is a work of fiction. Names, characters, business places, events and incidents are either the product of the author's imagination, or used in a fictitious manner. Any resemblance to actual persons, living or dead, or actual events is purely coincidental.

Lycan Valley Press Publications
1621 E 72nd ST STE 441 PMB15
Tacoma, Washington 98404 United States of America

Printed in the United States of America

First Edition, October 2020

ISBN 13: 978-1-645-62969-6

As yet, I'm unable to craft and deliver a story in isolation. Thank you to LVP Publications for their patience and support in bringing this work into the light of day. Thanks also to my beta readers Terri, Av, Pat and Kelly: my MVCs and heavy hitters. To the silent partners Nella and the Queen Bea, who are always down to talk game and the art of a good story, among other things. And also to Tom Mavroudis, Andrew Wilmot, Dion Winton-Polak, and Eric Ian Steele.

Cuzn: check tha résumé. You ain't seen a damned thing yet.

PART 1

C.C. ADAMS

Holloway, North London
18/03/2016, 15:12

Walking past the red-and-white traffic barrier, following the kerb and its double yellow line, Alice came to a stop at the end of the road, the complex of red brick and grey roofing now behind her.

Freedom. It had been a long time coming.

To look back now would be a cliché and, truth be told, she was glad to be shot of the place. As it was, her purse had somehow been mislaid, making her half an hour late by the time the purse was found. Alice allowed herself a rueful smile of both relief and anxiety. Outside was mostly deserted now, apart from a white van and a few cars.

Grey sky overhead suggested rain would come, while the chill air smelled fresh. Alice inhaled deeply, her eyes watering a little when the inside of her nose stung. Still, it beat the musty air she was used to. *What a fucking shithole.*

A flashing of light caught her eye. Another

double flash; all coming from a blue four-door hatchback parked three vehicles to her right. Alice made her way over and opened the passenger door, apprehension dissipating.

Naomi, one hand on the steering wheel, gave a gentle smile from under a dark glossy bob. "Hey," she said softly.

No more was needed—now was not the time for glib. Alice returned the smile and got in, the women exchanging pleasantries before Alice fastened her seatbelt and heaved a sigh of relief.

Naomi peeled the car away from the kerb and, weaving through back streets, pulled into Clapham some time later, easing the car along a tree-dotted street before parking and exiting outside a terraced house. "We're here," Naomi said, gesturing at the house.

Alice let herself out and looked across the roof of the car at the house. As far as she could tell, the property was well-kept: the front garden was paved, the walls were clean with white paint and red brick underneath. No visible signs of disrepair. "You bought it?"

Naomi shook her head. "No, renting. But it's a pretty good deal. I get the ground floor flat, and there's a couple, newlyweds, who I think have been here for around the last eight months. Quiet couple. Either that or the soundproofing is good," she quipped, a smile tugging one corner of her mouth.

"Uh-huh." Alice's gaze trailed over the upper

part of the house, one side shielded by branches of a nearby tree. It really did look beautiful. More than beautiful, it looked… Alice narrowed her gaze as she rummaged for the word. *Tranquil*, that was it. The house looked beautiful and tranquil, and right now, that was just what the doctor ordered.

"Hey, you hungry?"

Reverie melting away, Alice turned back to Naomi.

"You hungry?" Naomi repeated.

"Yeah, sure," she said, ambling around the front of the car and following Naomi as she let herself in. Alice closed the door behind her softly, noting a subtle hint of perfume in the air as she trailed behind Naomi, going down the hallway and entering through the door on the right. The smell was a little stronger—

Cheers erupted from a number of people seated around a table in the middle of the room, grinning upon Alice's entrance. One of the men stuck his forefinger and thumb in his mouth and blew a sharp whistle. Some of the party clapped.

Smiling in spite of herself, Alice clapped a hand to her chest while shooting a sidelong glance at Naomi. "You had something to do with this?"

Naomi bit the corner of her lip, restraining a smile. "I might have had a hand in it."

Alice bowed her head a little, momentarily overcome with shyness. A number of takeout cartons sat on the table, the open ones revealing fried rice and dim sum. Several bottles of spirits and soft drinks stood close by, along with empty glasses. One by one, Alice made her way around the group and conveyed her thanks: to their friend Richard, tall and stocky with a boyish smile and permanent bed-hair; to Naomi's Japanese boyfriend Kazu; and to Naomi's platinum-blonde friend Celeste.

Naomi seated herself and, meeting Alice's gaze, tipped her head to the only remaining seat at the table. Alice pulled out her chair and sat down, conscious of several pairs of eyes tracking her every move. "Well. This isn't awkward at all," she said, prompting scattered laughs from those at the table. "Nobody's eating yet?"

Kazu spoke first. "We were waiting for the guest of honour. So now that you're here…" he said, a grin breaking across his features. Naomi shot him a sour look, at which he clapped a hand over hers without making eye contact.

"Look, look," Richard said, his hand up as if he were about to wave goodbye. "Maybe it's best we just tuck in now, rather than put the lady on the spot, guys." He glanced over at her and gave a nod of encouragement.

Alice sighed and forced a smile. None of this was going to be easy. "I know I've waited long enough," she said. "Dig in."

"Waitaminnit," Celeste said, grinning, "wait, wait, wait, wait, WAIT," the final 'wait' prompting surprise and chuckles from around the table. "I think now would be as good a time as any to propose a toast." Glasses were filled and raised. "Here's to... moving onwards and upwards," she said, tipping Alice a wink.

"I'll drink to that," Richard said, raising his glass. "Cheers."

Glasses raised and clinked, returning the toast before Alice gave a shrug of defeat and urged the group to dig in. So they did. Over a course of Chinese food, alcohol (and weed, courtesy of Richard), the group chatted about reality TV, recent football matches, the upcoming Olympics in Rio, and whether women should make the first move in dating. As the day wore into evening, members of the party took their leave until only Naomi and Alice remained.

"Well," Naomi said, once the two of them were alone. "How was that?"

Alice gave a little tilt of her head. "It was okay, I guess." Her gaze fell upon the table and the myriad of open cartons—some still with food in—that were left. One farther away from her still had half a portion of pork fried rice in it. Alice pulled it toward her and idly picked at it with her chopsticks.

"Too much?"

Alice looked up.

"I mean..." Naomi paused. Pulled a rictus grin as she searched for the words. "Was all of this too much too soon?"

Was it? Alice shook her head. "No, it's not that. I

mean the food was great and everything. It's been too damned long since I had any kind of takeout." She tapped a fingernail against the carton in front of her. "You spared no expense, I see. I've already had one carton, I couldn't manage another!" She grinned, and then grew solemn. "But…"

Naomi folded her arms. "But you're feeling out of place?"

Alice drew her arms off the table and clasped her hands in her lap. "Yeah, I am."

That was all that would come for now, and that was all that needed to be said. For the last two years, there had been a preset structure of what to do and what *not* to do. Outside prison walls, the *reality* of choice rather than the ideal proved overwhelming.

"Come on," Naomi said softly. "You've not even been outside a full day. As much as you might want it, you… you won't adjust overnight. Just like you had to adjust to life on the inside, now you need to adjust to life on the outside, right? Do you want to go back?"

Alice shot Naomi a sour look. "Are you mad?"

"Well, there you go," Naomi said, poking an emphatic finger into the table and wedging a rice grain under her nail in the process. "Shit," she muttered, absently picking it out with another fingernail. "Obviously, you don't want to go back, so here's where you make a fresh start of it. *Right?* Right. Put all that crap behind you. There's a lot of opportunity ahead, and"—she leaned forward, pointing a finger—"it's Rebecca's wedding soon. When is it, again?"

Alice exhaled a short sigh. Naomi made a good point; hell, the wedding had clean skipped her mind. "In a few weeks."

"You didn't want to see her when you got out?" Naomi asked, her tone softer.

Alice chewed this over. "It's hard to explain. I wanted to see her, but I wasn't sure how it would go, you know? It might be too awkward. I know how Mum feels, anyway," she added, with an eye-roll. "She made that clear as crystal."

"Mmmm, maybe that's a battle lost. But Rebecca wants to see you."

A wry smile from Alice. "Yeah, she said so, once or twice."

"There you go. Didn't you say she even pushed the wedding back until after your release?"

Alice, lips pursed, nodded.

"Well, there you go. If she's letting you have that space now, it's because she understands what you're feeling, and accepts it as well. It gives you some time to get yourself back on your feet which is what you need—which is what *anyone* would need." Again with the forefinger.

"Yeah, you're right." Alice leaned back in her chair and folded her arms. "You're right," she said, her tone one of resignation. She gave a shrug.

"Of course I'm right."

Alice gave a slow nod.

Naomi grew solemn. "Buuuut…?"

There really wasn't an easy way to say it. "I don't have any idea where to start."

Naomi's gaze narrowed as she shifted in her seat. Alice couldn't help but notice the shorter woman's curvy figure and think on how her own must have changed in prison. What pounds she must have cursed before sentencing, she would probably kill for now.

"I have an idea," Naomi began, and from the tone, it became clear to Alice that whatever the idea might be, it wouldn't be open to debate. "I'll help you look for a job, which you'll use to pay half the rent here. How does that sound so far?"

"So far?" For Alice, the hard part was over: she had a roof over her head and a helping hand to get a job. She clenched her jaw, biting back any outward trace of triumph.

"There are conditions."

Conditions. Not expected, but understandable. "Go on."

"First," Naomi said, holding up her little finger, "you'll look for work every day, with no exceptions. I'll help, sure, but you need to start helping yourself."

"Okay."

"Second," Naomi continued, holding up the adjacent finger, "you'll pick up the place while I'm not here. That means helping me with the cooking and cleaning, on top of you looking for a job.

Third," she said, now holding up three fingers and waving her hand back and forth for emphasis. "Third. If there's any drama that follows you here, *any drama at all*, you move out immediately. You're not bringing any of that crap into my home or my life, okay?"

As harsh as it may have sounded, Alice couldn't help but concede that Naomi had a point. Memories of Leon came to mind; Leon who had apparently shoved Naomi to the floor, demanding the whereabouts of on / off-girlfriend Alice, even though Naomi had no idea where Alice may have been. One of several instances where trust had been worn down. Right now was as good a time as any to start repairing that trust.

Alice held out her hand. "Deal. Thank you," she said, her smile bashful.

Naomi reached out and gave Alice's hand a firm shake. "You're welcome. You've probably had a long day, and it might even be a long night." She rose to clear the table, leaving the remaining half-carton of pork fried rice and a bottle of Baileys. "The spare room's already made up. If I were you, I'd get some sleep. You've got a busy day ahead tomorrow."

'Busy day ahead' was an understatement. Everything from sifting through page after page of old emails to checking accounts with a number of service providers. Snail mail was still an issue, and it seemed no business would drop the pursuit of a potential customer, even if that pursuit ran for two years. With the benefit of hindsight, Alice would label this as her easiest day since her release. Rather than feeling listless, clearing the driftwood of her imprisonment gave her a degree of focus. And yet, it was nowhere near as daunting as what lay ahead.

Two weeks and five days. In those two weeks and five days, Naomi helped Alice polish and hone her CV, and kept her ear to the ground for any possible job openings. Unlike many friends who would pore over jobsites and chase up recruitment agencies, Naomi had enough savvy to recognise the value of networking in the job hunt. Alice, not in a position to be choosy, had tried every method at her disposal, though each instance of a telephone interview or face-to-face interview had resulted in a curt and formal letter declining her application. Alice found herself cursing the word 'unfortunately', telling it and the email it was typed in to go fuck itself. Naomi wouldn't let on at her own frustration. One, because Alice needed the support, and two, because Naomi needed to keep her own focus to help Alice get a job. In this way, Alice could help pay rent (which wasn't cheap) and so Naomi would protect her investment.

Networking and persistence finally paid off when a friend of a friend got Alice a job on the Lancôme perfumery and cosmetics counter in Debenhams on Oxford Street. Glass counters full of perfumes and cosmetics lay in open squares for sales assistants in makeup chic to operate from. Square pillars stretched from floor to ceiling and wore glossy pictures of models and A-list actresses. Now, blonde hair ponytailed, Alice's working days included a black blazer with matching skirt and black kitten heels, which slid across the department's glassy tiling. The sheer variety of product, from Bobbi Brown to Yves Saint Laurent, was overwhelming at first—shit, just one company would cover a lot of range in their square. Days grew easier as Alice learned the layout of the department, from the slanted racks of lipstick and blusher to the sleek steel high chairs that women seated themselves in for partial makeovers. It took some getting used to, but Alice was determined to make a go of it, and the staff on her counter were helpful enough.

Most of them.

With Fumi, what Alice didn't like was the girl's unflinching look. Had it been a glare, Alice would have known how to handle it, but the girl would just give her a blank look, which was too measured, too controlled. As if there were some monologue that the black girl wanted to spit at Alice about her past. Trying to engage her in conversation met with monosyllabic answers, if they were verbal at all.

"Okay," Alice said, turning back to the centre of the counter and facing Fumi. "That's me done."

Carrie, a thin twenty-something brunette peered from behind Fumi's back. "All done?" Seven years in London hadn't quite erased the Kiwi accent.

Alice nodded. "All done."

"Good one. We'll see you tomorrow," she said, giving a nod.

"Will do. Bye." Alice turned to the black girl, whose gaze was levelled back at her, unblinking like a snake hunting a mouse. "Bye, Fumi."

Still the same gaze. "Bye."

For all the hubbub in the crowd, the tone of that one word fell flat; useless and without warmth or meaning. Alice forced herself to walk past the pair at a casual pace, seeing in her mind's eye how she would grab that stupid little shit by her neck and choke the life out of her. The old, quick-tempered Alice would have bent to that frustration. The same frustration remained even after Alice had collected her bag from the staff room, woven a path through the department, and headed outside. Alice moved away from the entrance and back up to the glass front of the store. Under the marquee that ran the length of the store, the sun of the late afternoon cast warmth across her from the chest down, strobed by the sheer volume of shoppers, tourists and the like.

Alice sighed and looked up from under the marquee. Less than a month ago, she wouldn't even have had this kind of view, let alone this kind of freedom. Just a pokey beige cell with a high window. Yeah, life in cosmetics was an improvement.

Yeah, right.

Fucking stupid little shit.

Alice waited for an opening, then pushed away from the glass and fell in step with the crowd.

Fumilola, the lowlife stupid little shit.

Even from one of the earliest encounters, Alice had stomached enough of the passive-aggressive and confronted the girl outright, asking if the girl had a problem with her. Fumi's response had been indifferent: "You're not my problem." Alice's immediate reaction was nausea, at having provoked such clinical contempt in someone. Fury came next: the indignation that some little girl had the gall to dismiss her like shit smeared across the sole of her shoe. It was fucking arrogant and disrespectful. By rights, Alice should have—

"Careful, you nearly hit me."

Alice looked up.

A moment of shock; enough time to shift to automatic pilot.

Kieran?

He stood watchful in front of her, hooking his thumbs into his back pockets. On first impression, Kieran didn't look a whole lot different from the last time Alice saw him... except now he was in a paisley print shirt, jeans and shoes: a more colourful wardrobe. Thick black hair teased into spikes, with a trace of stubble lining his jaw.

"Hello." His brow lifted, leaving his expression less stern.

"Oh," she said, looking about her to make sure

she didn't block too many pedestrians. "It's just been that kind of a day."

No answer.

She opened her mouth. Paused. This wasn't the best day, and she'd sure as hell had some shitty ones since her release. "Okay, so maybe not the best day so far."

Kieran curled his lip, nostrils flaring as he did so. At last, he beckoned toward the glass front of the store with a tilt of his head, and he and Alice moved toward it, away from the tide of pedestrians. Alice barely missed a couple of Italian girls barrelling into her, one of whom lost her grip on her iPhone. Her friend flung out a dextrous hand and clapped it against her side, saving it from shattering on concrete. Both girls giggled in relief as they righted the phone and moved on.

"So," Kieran said, leaning back against the glass once they had taken up position. "How's life been treating you?"

Alice searched his face. He looked at her with an expression of mild intrigue and nothing more. As for his features, he looked pretty much the same as he did two or so years ago except for the slitted gaze, as though even the shade was too bright. Or maybe he was genuinely curious.

"I've been working," she said at last. "On the Lancôme counter back at Debenhams."

"Really?" He turned bodily toward her. "Never thought you'd go in for make-up and stuff like that."

"What are you trying to say?" she said, peering at him, and he held up his hands in mock surrender.

Levity was good. But it barely scratched the surface. Alice cast a glance across the street. People bustled as traffic slowed for aimless pedestrians, one car creeping forward only to be halted by an amber light turning red. Alice turned back to Kieran, bracing herself.

"I was released a couple of weeks ago," she said.

His smile dimmed as his brows twitched in a questioning frown, and his chest rose in a silent sigh. "I can see that."

Shit. This wasn't going to be easy at all. "Exactly," Alice continued. "Still, I'm making a go of things as best as I can, now that I'm back in the world. Not without its challenges, but…"

Kieran's look of nonchalance gave nothing away.

Awkward silence.

"Anyway," Alice said, her tone resigned. "What are you doing around here? You're shopping?"

A ghost of a smile flitted across his face and for a moment, Alice remembered the roguish charm of days long past, duvet Sundays and Dutch ovens. "No, nothing glamourous," he said. "My dentist is actually at the back of the store, much further down. You've heard of Harley Street, right?"

"With all the expensive doctors and medical care?"

"Something like that. Wimpole Street is close by. Not doctors, but all dentists, orthodontists, implantologists. Teeth doctors, basically. I thought I might have chipped a tooth, but no, crisis averted."

Alice peered at him and he curled his lip back from his teeth. Those teeth were still a *liiiiiittle* yellow (since a history of smoking would do that), but apart from a couple of lower incisors looking stepped, Kieran's teeth looked even. "They look fine to me," she said, at which Kieran gave a slight bow and mouthed a thank-you.

"You look like you could use a drink." That slitted gaze of curiosity returned and Kieran cocked his head, lips parting. "Wanna go get one?"

Alice flinched. "What?"

"Yeah. Now, if now's good."

"Why?"

Kieran pursed his lips as his eyes slid closed for a moment. "Look," he said at last. "I've tried not to hold a grudge for the past. Easier said than done, I'll admit, but I've tried not to. Regardless of how you might describe life back on the outside, you look like you've taken a battering. So believe it or not, I'm actually down to listen. Call it a drink to bury any hatchet. Or at the very least, a free drink on me."

Alice huffed in disgust. "Really? Why would you even talk to me now, after everything else?"

His gaze hardened. "*Because* I try not to waste energy holding a grudge. On top of that, you look like you've had a really shitty day and could use a drink. Plus, I know a cool bar from around here, which doesn't get too crowded at all. So," he said, forcing congeniality back in place. "Shall we?"

Kieran may have been trusting to a fault (and if *she* was, Alice thought ruefully, maybe she wouldn't have gotten herself in this fucking mess in the first place), but he made a persuasive argument. And like any ex-partner, there were some traits of your personality that they could still read like an open book. She relented, allowing Kieran to lead her away from the crowds, following a backroads route toward Tottenham Court Road until they came to a large bar on the corner with a neon-lit marquee. Heavy canvas parasols with "Black & Blue" stamped on each hexagonal side stood over patio tables and chairs, while a giant bronze statue of a bull faced out across the street. Alice slowed as she approached the statue. Her head fell in line with the base of the statue's jaw.

"Black & Blue?" she asked. The expression on the statue was stern from this angle.

"Typical bar," Kieran said, drawing close to her. "Some canapés, a steak or two, and not forgetting they serve alcohol." He led her inside where a black-shirted waitress beamed at them as she clasped her hands on her apron. Kieran led Alice past round tables topped with white tablecloths and gleaming silverware, before they drew up to the bar at the far end of the room. He placed an order of a bottle of cider and a vodka tonic with the nearest barman, then ushered Alice to one of the tall tables in the far corner, waiting for Alice to seat herself before following suit. Kieran took a swig of his cider.

"Not my weapon of choice," he said ruefully. "I'm a Kopparberg man myself."

"What, no… what was it?"

"Bulmers?" He gave a wry smile. "Not anymore."

Alice peered at the bottle. "And what's that?"

Kieran twisted his wrist, looking at the label. "Rekorderlig. Some places have it, but it's not as clean as a Kopparberg, in my opinion." He took another swig and set the bottle down. "Anyhow. We didn't come here just to talk about my taste in beverages. Tell me what's new with you."

Over the course of four more vodka tonics, Alice did just that. Even though she initially had misgivings about going for a drink with Kieran of all people, there was something cathartic about unloading your thoughts on a stranger (or in this case, a relative one). Over the next hour and a half, Alice had not only given him an overview of what life in prison had been like, but she had also told him about how it had taken a toll on her, how awkward it felt to be back in the real world, as well as the joy in her life such as Rebecca's upcoming wedding. In turn, Kieran had touched on his career move from mobile telecoms to wine and bespoke cellar solutions, along with a growing interest in languages. By now, more customers were in the bar: from men wearing sharp multi-hued shirts open at the collar to women in skirts or tight jeans, with fresh lipstick and high heels.

Alice took a sip of her drink and braced her hand against the table's edge. Closing her eyes for a moment, she forced herself to breathe slowly.

"Are you okay?"

"Sure, I'm okay," she said, fixing him with a surly look. "Why wouldn't I be?"

His lips curved in a faint trace of a smile. "It's just that you've had a few drinks. You're having a hard time focusing, it seems."

"Don't worry about it," she said, fluttering a hand at him. "You just worry about yourself." With that, she returned to her drink, watching effervescence in the glass, watching *anything* to lose the sensation of his eyes upon her. At last she looked up, returned her drink to the table and scanned the room. Not only was there more commotion in the bar, but… but… Something looked odd, but she couldn't put her finger on it. A number of women talking to a number of men. "What's going on?" she wondered aloud.

Kieran, his eyes half-lidded, lifted his chin. "It's a speed-dating session." Alice turned to him and he gave a squint in a facial shrug. "Well, the actual speed dating is downstairs, but when they want to take a break or when the session is over, they come upstairs."

Alice looked over his shoulder, seeing a staircase leading to a lower floor. Yes, now she could hear chatter from downstairs. "That explains it, I guess."

Kieran didn't respond but his expression

resembled that of someone pleasuring himself under the table... except his arms were folded, in full view.

"You're okay?" It came out harsher than she intended, but right now, she was too drunk to care.

"Yeah," he breathed. He nodded in the direction of the staircase. "Sounds like fun."

"And this isn't?"

He turned his attention back to her, and cocked his head to one side.

"I didn't ask you to come here, did I?"

His smile dimmed. A muscle in his jaw clenched, and his lips parted. He exhaled a breath as he watched her. Around them, the crowd continued to chatter and laugh. "No, I offered to lend an ear. Did it ever occur to you," he said coolly, "that it's not all about you? That your actions don't affect just you?"

"Kieran, what the fuck?" she snapped. "I mean, seriously, what the actual fuck? You invite me for a drink just so you can have a front-row seat to gloat, is that it?"

"That's what you really think?" he asked, and for the first time since she saw him earlier, Alice could see *disgust* written over his face. "The answer's 'no.'" He leaned forward on the table, rocking it a little as he did so. "But if I wanted to, maybe you deserve it," he said, eyebrows raised for emphasis.

That did it.

Alice snatched up her glass and tossed the drink at him. Vodka tonic sloshed Kieran in the face and wet his shirtfront in a clinging bib, as ice cubes hit the floor, skittering. At the adjacent table, two men looked back over their shoulders, and a ponytailed woman peered out from behind one of them.

"How about that?" Alice said, gesturing at the onlookers. "Now you've got yourself a bigger audience. That should make you happy, right? *Right?*" She eased herself off her stool and strode out of the bar without as much as a backward glance.

Leaving Kieran with his head low over the table, the drink on his shirt clinging wet and cold against his skin.

Around him, background conversation began to pick up, as did the myriad of footsteps from one table to the next, men using their most subtle manoeuvres to get closer to the women, the creaks of taut stool cushions as women positioned themselves to better face (or shun) the next suitor. The smell of wine in the air. Kieran curled his lip and drummed his fingers on the table, a slow and rhythmic cadence.

Alice.

Still his fingers drummed.

He slid his hand off the table and underneath to the table's trunk, gripping it in his palm. Cold metal, but not cold enough.

Ahead of him, a conversation about the

upcoming Olympics in Rio. Somewhere off to his right, another conversation on the virtues of searing meat before putting it in the oven. Feminine voices discussing sales techniques in the workplace and the stumbling blocks that came early in a career. The clink of glasses on a table. The scrape of a shoe on black marbled flooring—and Kieran grit his teeth. Background music: some crooning sax played in a faux attempt at cool. Inane giggling. Empty bottles clinking in a bin behind the bar—

Growling, Kieran slid off his bar stool and walked outside. From this exit, he found himself at the adjacent end of the patio garden in blessed quiet, the bull statue around the corner to his right at the adjacent entrance. Along with a handful of pedestrians looking to avoid the crowds clogging the high street, the occasional vehicle of some savvy driver avoiding the main road made a turn around the crossroad.

Kieran looked up. A cloudless navy-blue sky, with a winking speck of light cutting a slow and steady path across it.

He clenched his jaw and hung his head.

Alice.

Under a far table, a pigeon strutted an ambling path from its flock before veering past him. As the bird drew closer, he tracked its movement. Those stupid orange eyes were wide open as if to see everything, but worked for a brain too simple to compute the input.

In one smooth move, Kieran dropped to a crouch and shot out a hand, catching the bird around its neck. Wings pushed and fluttered against his fist. Still those stupid orange eyes, expressionless, incapable of conveying any reasoning or argument for release. *Stupid, stupid, stupid.*

Kieran brought his arm up and clenched his fist hard. Avian bones crunched and crackled as the wings fell limp, the feathery body hanging loose against his wrist.

Still Kieran sat in a crouch.

Something began to trickle inside his palm.

Scent, warm and ferric seeped between his fingers, stilling him. Lips parted, as if an answer was on the tip of his tongue.

…no.

A sigh though a clenched jaw.

He got to his feet and tossed the bird aside, where it landed on hard paving with a muffled clap. The worst part, he thought, was that it would have to be a bird for now. Bigger prey would attract more attention.

Bigger prey.

He shoved his hands into his pockets, cursing under his breath at the slickness that soaked from his palm through his trousers. Nothing else to do this night except head home.

The scent was immediate as soon as Alice opened the door. Rich pastry and hot savoury meat. She let herself in and followed the smell into the lounge. Naomi looked up from a plateful of pie and baked beans. Half a pie.

"Hi," she said, at which Naomi returned her greeting. "Mmmmm. Something smells good," she said, eyeing the plate. "What is it?"

"Steak and kidney. Go grab the other half from the microwave."

For this, Alice needed no invitation, and soon the two ladies were both seated and eating, with a Baileys and cream close at hand for Alice.

"You've been out?" Naomi asked.

Alice nodded. No doubt the alcohol stunk on her. She swallowed a mouthful of pie. "Correction. I've not only been out, I was taken out."

"Oh, really?" Naomi asked, her tone brightening. "By who?"

Alice glanced up, and locked eyes with Naomi.

"Really?" A somewhat fatuous smile now. "Who?"

"A blast from the past."

"Oh, it's like that now? Okay." Naomi bit her lip as she sat back in her chair, miming like she was in the middle of some complex calculation. "Marcus."

"No."

"Okay. My next guesses are 'give up' and 'give up.' Just tell me. Seriously."

"Okay." She feigned a look of indifference. "It

was Kieran."

Naomi blinked. "Wait a minute. *The* Kieran?"

"*The* Kieran."

"What are you doing, going out with him?"

"I ran into him when I was finishing work. He said I looked like I had a bad day, so he invited me out for a drink." Alice turned her attention to her glass, and took another sip. At this rate, the inside of her arteries would be clogged like a public toilet.

"You're telling me that after everything that's happened, the guy just decides to take you for a drink?" Naomi shot her a look of disgust.

Alice sucked in her cheeks and savoured the hit of cream. "You know, that's what I thought. But to be fair, Kieran has always been…" She fluttered her hand. "What's the word? A giver. Yeah—he's always been a giver." She shrugged one shoulder. "Maybe that's why I fell for him in the first place."

"Fine, so he took you for a drink. What else?"

Alice gripped her knife harder. "I asked him if he was happy."

The look of bewilderment on Naomi's face spoke volumes.

"Then I threw my drink on him and left."

"As you do."

Alice gave a sheepish look and waited for the penny to drop.

Naomi shook her head in confusion, disgust creasing her features. "What? Are you mad?"

"What do you mean, mad?"

Naomi held up a forestalling hand. "Let me see if I get this right so far. You drag his name through the mud. Which backfires on you. Sucks to be you, but, hey. You then happen to run into him once you're back outside, and he offers to take you for a drink— all in aid of mending fences. How do you repay him? You throw a drink on him." She massaged her temple with tapered fingertips. "Seems like he's the one who should be throwing the drink."

"So now you're taking his side."

"No, I'm not taking 'his' side," Naomi groaned. "I'm taking the side of what's right, and what you just did was wrong. No two ways about it."

Alice folded her arms.

"Maybe try and think *before* you act?!"

Alice paused. Granted, Naomi could show a quick temper: the time when FunkiNecta door staff told them the club was full, only to let in two slinky young girls moments later—that was a prime example. But this?

Again, Naomi held up a hand. "Look. I don't deny that time inside may have been rough for you, but remember that it was your actions that put you there. Some may say deservedly so, but that's not the issue here. The issue is that someone took time out to listen to your woes, and this is how you repay them. Poor judgement on your part."

Embarrassment now. No, not just embarrassment, but *shame*. Arms still folded, Alice hung her head. Beneath the ticking of the wall-clock, the weight of silence hung on her like a blanket, smothering her. Her cheeks heated. *What an almighty fuck-up.* The weight of Naomi's gaze hung on her too. Alice couldn't see it, but she could sure as shit feel it.

Head low, she inhaled. "I'm sorry," she said softly.

"Yes, but it's not me you should be apologising to."

Alice wondered if her neck would still ache like this if she wasn't so fucking ashamed. She looked up, and saw only exasperation on her friend's face. "Do you think I should go and apologise?"

"God, no!" At this, Naomi clapped her palms on the table. "What's the matter with you, are you mad? After what you've just done, what makes you think this man wants to lay eyes on you again? Seriously."

More shame now. "I... should probably apologise and try to—"

"No," Naomi said, her tone questioning, but thick with derision. "If I were you, I'd steer clear of him. Good intentions or bad. I think you've done more than enough damage for one man. Leave it alone." She returned to the rest of her meal and ate in silence. Reluctantly, Alice followed suit.

The rest of the evening followed in the same fashion, and apart from a cursory goodnight, they retired to their rooms in silence. Alice lay awake in bed, staring at the ceiling and trying to ignore the lampshade that hung from its centre, marring an otherwise blank canvas. Minutes after she had gotten into bed, the lamp had hung in her blind spot, further aided by the gloom in the room and the darkness of night outside her window. Now she could see it all too clearly, further keeping her awake, as did her thoughts. Those same thoughts plagued her into an eventual sleep.

Through a crisp and cool morning, a white sun blurred behind a grey sky.

Through a humdrum day.

Through a tense afternoon.

Once her shift had finished, Alice visited Clinton Cards further down Oxford Street from Debenhams. After spending the better part of half an hour looking for something that hit the right note, she decided against it. She headed into the bowels of Oxford Circus tube station, almost taking the Victoria line southbound out of habit. Thankfully the journey was short, given the time of evening, and by the time she reached Maida Vale, it wasn't even seven o'clock yet. She made her way out of the station and paused to take in her surroundings. Everything about the area looked old. The burgundy tiling of the station exterior looked old. The font of lettering on the station façade that said, "Station" and "Entrance" looked old. The scaffolding barricaded by blue metal sheeting, underscoring that some old things needed renovation. But the neighbouring buildings—an assortment of greying brick with arched windows—

those were old too. Alice wove her way through an array of back streets before entering at one end of a street of terraced houses. Unlike the houses in southern areas of the city such as her Clapham, some housing in Maida Vale was built as flats (known locally as mansion blocks). Where those southern redbrick houses would be two storeys high, these grey-green buildings would be two and a half-storeys, where the uppermost floor was a loft conversion. As such, those houses always looked a little odd to Alice, because while there was an extra floor of windows, those on the top looked shorter (and sillier).

Alice slowed as she walked down the street, her gaze sliding over the trees, their crusted and flaking bark, and their roots that lifted and fractured the slabs of the pavement. She stopped before a line of heavy black railings and pushed open the gate, climbing the steps to a blue door. On the right hand side of the doorway, an intercom with three buttons. She laid her palm against the top of the intercom. Was she really going to do this? She pushed harder on the heel of her palm, feeling the corner of the intercom bite into the flesh. Still, she hadn't come all this way for nothing.

Hand resting on the intercom, she lifted her thumb and jabbed one of the buttons. A distant buzz sounded from inside the property.

Alice waited. Streets away, traffic rolled by, uninterested, and the occasional car drove along the street, none slowing to visit anyone or to see what Alice was doing. Minutes passed.

Alice took a few steps back and looked up at the house. No lights were on, although, given the warm glow in the blue sky overhead, the evening didn't need artificial light just yet. On a day like this, it was possible that people were sat in pubs, leisurely working their way through pints of lager. Kieran liked a drink for sure, but he was never the type who would make a beeline to a pub in order to get one. Bars were more his speed.

She stepped back up to the door and tried the buzzer again. And again, minutes passed without any discernible response. Not quite the outcome she was waiting for.

Hmmmmm…

She rested a hand against the letterbox and lifted the flap inward on her fingertips as she bent. From here, she couldn't see much, apart from a beige carpeted hallway, and the legs of a wall table, no doubt with an assortment of mail atop it. Not too different from the last—

"Seriously?"

Alice spun on her heel. Kieran drew up alongside the gate, a jacket slung over his arm. With his free hand, he felt for the gate and paced toward her, his leather uppers soundless, his eyes never leaving Alice's. "What are you doing here?" Unlike the previous evening, Kieran's lips (his lower lip a little fuller than the top) curled in annoyance. He continued to stare, unblinking.

"I, uhhh…" She swallowed, her mouth dry.

He drew closer and Alice took an involuntary step back, until she chided herself to get a grip. Pulse racing, she stood her ground. Kieran came closer until their noses were almost touching.

"You're on my territory."

Alice blinked. "Sorry?"

He growled in his chest.

"Kieran, listen. I did a bad thing yesterday. Insult to injury, given what I've already done to you." She paused, noting how his head wove sideways ever so slightly, as though he were listening to or smelling for something. "I came to apologise. Maybe I have no right to, but I wanted to make amends, like you did. If you were to tell me to go fuck myself, you'd totally have that right. But I'm sorry." She folded her arms, cupping her elbows in her hands.

"Well," Kieran said, his tone cordial now. "I thank you for taking the time to come out here and tell me, but I really couldn't give a shit. So I suggest you take that apology of yours and use it to go fuck yourself."

Alice recoiled. On offering Kieran the opportunity, she hadn't expected that he would take it. From what she knew of him, or rather what she *remembered* of him, he had been the easygoing type where she was concerned, often conceding for momentary peace. "Okay, maybe I was out of line, so the least I could do was try to make amends—

remember, I didn't have to come out here. But if you can't accept that, then I can't help you." Still with folded arms, she gave a shrug before she turned on her heel and headed to the gate. Kieran started to follow her, but a glare in his direction caught him short. "You know," she said. "I'm not perfect, but I'm least I'm trying to move on with my life. You should try doing the same." With a look of disappointment, she swung the gate shut behind her, the heavy iron clanging in the frame of the railing.

Once he saw her disappear at the end of the street, Kieran turned his attention back to his front door and let himself into his flat, heading to the room behind the lounge. Twin steel hoops sat yards apart in the centre of the room, partly embedded in bare concrete flooring, with a mass of shipyard chain piled nearby. Dingy mattresses laid slanted against the walls. Kieran seated himself cross-legged before one of the hoops and gripped it in both hands, his head hung low over his lap. Cold from the floor leached through the fabric of his trousers while sweat began to leak from his pores, sticking the back of his shirt to him. His grip on the hoop tightened, his knuckles now standing out in pale relief on his fists. The cold. A poor substitute, but right now, it would take the edge off.

"Lemon chicken and boiled rice?"

Alice pointed across the table. "That's hers."

The waiter, a slim and quiff-haired Asian, lifted the plate of lemon chicken from his forearm and set it in front of Rebecca. "And chicken, ginger, spring onion and egg fried rice."

"Right here," Alice said, inhaling. Damn, it smelled good.

The waiter bid them enjoy before weaving a path through tables and back toward the kitchen.

Rebecca leaned forward conspiratorially over her plate. "What're you waiting for? Dig in, hon."

Alice grinned and dug up a forkful of rice, savouring the freshness and the fried egg. She never could get enough of the egg. The crispy roll starters took the edge off, but they too were part of the main event. Lunch with Rebecca—another pleasure she hadn't enjoyed in far too long. In a decent place too, from the light blue table cloth to ornate Chinese lanterns overhead, and ceiling-to-floor windows around the expansive seating area, ensuring as much natural light as possible. Not surprising that most tables were occupied. As far as Alice was aware, Poons had long since closed its few branches dotted throughout the London area, yet Rebecca had simply told her that was where the next lunch date would be. Now, on one of the back streets between Oxford Circus and Tottenham Court Road, Alice put her half-day to good use and grabbed lunch with her big sister. Even better that her big sister was paying the bill. Money didn't factor in as such: it was simply nice to be treated and pampered. Becca could always be relied upon for that. Leaner in the face and with hair a shade darker than Alice's, Rebecca could also be relied upon to turn heads, as well as ignore them.

"How's the food?" Rebecca asked after a few mouthfuls.

"Mmmmm, good. Really good." Alice held up her glass. "Thank you."

Rebecca clinked her glass with Alice's. "Any time."

Eating in silence, background chatter coming from other diners, as did the clank and clatter of silverware and chopsticks on plates.

Then, "We'll have to get you measured up at some point."

Alice nodded without looking up. Of course she needed to be measured; after all, it wouldn't do to have any dress split, much less a bridesmaid's dress.

"Are you bringing a plus one?"

"No," Alice said around a mouthful of rice. "Not yet, anyway."

"Still easing back in?" Alice looked up at Rebecca, her smile somewhat wistful. "Nothing wrong with taking your time. It'll happen when you're good and ready."

Alice opened her mouth to say something, only to see Rebecca's gaze narrow across the table, her smile still in place. Wordlessly, Rebecca slid her hand across the table to Alice's and laced fingers with her sister. Alice looked her sister in the eye and tightened her grip on Rebecca's hand. "Really. Thank you."

"You're welcome."

They broke contact after a while. "So," Rebecca said. "Any idea how you're getting to the venue? You know this is one time where I can't give you a lift."

Alice gasped in mock indignation. "That was a low blow."

"No," Rebecca replied, gesturing with her wine glass. "That was a *true* blow. So again, I ask: how are you getting to the venue?"

"Where's the venue again?"

"It's at the Bingham Hotel in Richmond. Forgotten again, have you?"

Alice shot her sister a sour expression, which earned another rising of eyebrows: *come on, then.*

"I don't know," she said, with a shrug. "Maybe I'll get a cab there." Their waiter returned to the table, hands clasped and asking if everything was okay, and then retreating with a smile upon the sisters' assurance that it was. Alice turned her attention back to Rebecca, her sister eyeing her above a sip of wine. "I'm sure I'll manage."

"I'm sure you will," Rebecca said. "It's a wedding. There should be a good turnout and besides, the same way that a lot of people may be driving, I'm sure there will be those that aren't. Just let me know if you want me to make some arrangement for you."

"Becca," Alice said, pushing back in her seat, "you shouldn't have to."

"No, I shouldn't." She deftly plucked a clump of rice in her chopsticks as she looked up. "So why do I? Hmmm?" She popped the rice into her mouth and gave it a slow chew, her gaze steady. "There might be a spare room or two at the Bingham. Might make things easier."

Alice ate some more; pursing her lips when she saw how little was left on her plate. She coughed a chuckle of amusement. *Hungrier than I thought.* No wonder: jacket potatoes at Her Majesty's Convenience weren't the height of fine dining. So why did she still feel so... *awkward*, back on the outside?

"Work okay?"

"Hmmm?"

Rebecca took another sip of wine, barely finishing before repeating the question. "Is work okay?"

Alice paused, then shrugged. "It's been better."

"Better how?"

Alice slowed her chewing. "It's been... it's been uphill. You could say I'm having trouble fitting in. Or more like the others have trouble accepting me."

"You mean your record?"

Alice nodded. "Partly. I mean it's not like I advertise what happened, but I'm sure that people will remember a name, or put two and two together, you know?"

"Hon," Rebecca said, shaking her head. "It was a bad choice, sure. But that's in the past. The best you can do now is move on, and if you're moving on, then for the most part, other people will follow suit. Just keep your head down and focus on your work. If you show them you're serious about facing up to your mistakes and then putting them behind you, people will soon start to follow suit. You'll see."

"Like Mum?"

Rebecca weighed this, the stem of her wine glass pinched between thumb and forefinger. Her eyelids closed briefly. "She'll come around. Especially on the day," she said. "It's family."

"You make it sound so easy."

"I hope not!" Rebecca said, eyes widening in a mock glare. "Not easy." She softened. "But not impossible, either."

Again, their hands met across the table, the fingers lacing together, stronger than before.

Far from the kitchen, across the tables and to the main entrance, scents, and sound of chatter kept the restaurant lively. Kieran stood in the doorway with his hands in his pockets. 'Bad choice' was an understatement. *Plus one?* The only plus one Alice deserved was a slap.

Kieran scanned the restaurant, eyebrows lifting

in resigned approval. The wood-beam ceiling adorned with authentic paper lanterns. The chopsticks used at pretty much every table. The hoi sin duck and dim sum served in the round bamboo steamer baskets, and the smell of good wine. More wait staff cut graceful paths between tables, offering to clear plates or top up wine. One waitress made her way to the reservations pedestal near the entrance.

"Did you want a table, sir?" she asked, clasping her hands on her pinafore.

Kieran gave a tight shake of the head. "Won't be necessary." He cast a sweeping look across the ceiling and the far reaches of the restaurant. "It seems like a great place. Do you mind if I take a business card for future reference?"

"No, not at all," the waitress replied, beaming. She plucked a card from a cardholder on the pedestal and handed it Kieran, who shook it in affirmation like he was ringing a bell. "Much appreciated," he said, turning to leave.

"Have a good day now."

The smile on his lips vanished once he was outside the door, and only by the time he was far from the restaurant and back on the main road had he started to unclench his jaw. The northbound commute home and even the airy cool of his cell did little to appease Kieran and he dumped himself on the swivel chair at his computer. Practised keystrokes brought him his homepage, then his search engine, and then his search. He clicked on one of the listed links, watching the circular swirl as the page loaded. Then:

Woman who cried rape is jailed for two years

Kieran curled his lip, his nostrils flaring.

The judge told Alice Morecambe, 34, who made the falsified claim against her ex-boyfriend Kieran Griffin after a row, that this had undermined the legal system's efforts to provide both justice and sympathy for rape victims.

The court also heard that Mr. Griffin was subjected to 'degrading and distressing' examinations while being held in police custody for no less than eight hours. As of last night, Mr. Griffin was unavailable for comment. Judge Malcolm Ewell said the investigation had wasted more than three thousand pounds of taxpayers' money and two hundred and fifty police man hours.

He added: 'The police invest much in giving sympathetic treatment to women who make genuine complaints of rape—which you knowingly abused. You have undermined and jeopardised the efforts that are being made to treat victims of rape properly, fairly and sympathetically. The offence in itself is serious. Not only may your actions bring distress and awful consequences for the accused, but there will be wider implications for those women who have been raped.'

Morecambe, a former nurse from Rainham, Essex, split from her fiancé once she discovered his infidelity, Basildon Crown Court heard. She began drinking heavily to cope with the rejection and using dating websites. In September 2007, she met Mr. Griffin, who worked for Carphone Warehouse, through the Plenty of Fish website. They began a relationship, but the court heard that she was also seeing at least one other man.

In January last year, the couple rowed after Mr. Griffin accused her of having another man at her home. As a result, Mr. Griffin ended the relationship and asked Miss Morecambe to move out, after which, Morecambe dialled 999 and accused Mr. Griffin of rape. He was arrested in front of his colleagues and taken to the police station.

Judge Ewell said: 'It was an extraordinary performance which involved deliberate untruths, as the jury found.'

The arrest itself was one of the more degrading episodes in the whole affair, and it wouldn't have been so bad were he actually guilty of anything. He remembered his first reaction at the time was bewilderment, and that given how often he cooked breakfast for her (with pan-fried mackerel, for fuck's sake), this was the last thing he would have expected. Her fucking someone else, sure, maybe: she always did love the attention. Enough that the hickey on the base of her neck couldn't be ignored with extra makeup, or protestations that she had taken a knock in a doorway.

Kieran backtracked a page and clicked on another entry:

> *Prison is "inevitable" for women who falsely cry rape because it "drives a nail" in to the rape conviction rate, senior judges have warned.*

A centred picture of a prisoner's-eye view from a cell preceded the following text:

> *The Court of Appeal said false allegations damage conviction rates of genuine rapes and are "terrifying" for innocent victims. The judges spoke out as they dismissed an appeal by a former nurse who was jailed for two years after falsely accusing a man she met on an online dating site…*

Memories of the first (but not the last) woman to spit at him came to mind, and he remembered balling his fist, only to see the woman's husband follow suit. The woman's husband, although a couple of inches shorter, looked like he outweighed Kieran by a good twenty pounds. Impotent fury and shame followed.

> *In the original trial, the court heard how Mr. Griffin was subjected to "degrading and upsetting" examinations while being held by police for ten hours*

following the rape claim.

Charles Hearne, the Liberal Democrat home affairs spokesman, said: "False rape allegations are an insult to genuine victims of this detestable crime and those who maliciously make such allegations should expect no less than the strongest penalty." However, Helen Thackeray, of Women Against Rape, said the sentence was "outrageous" and warned the judge's comments risked "putting women off reporting rapes."

"Bullshit," Kieran muttered through a sigh of derision, swivelling to and fro. Further articles followed a similar pattern, with the intro covering the sentencing and the background, and then opinions from either side of the argument for revealing defendant names before a verdict was returned, guilty or otherwise. Returning to a fresh search page, he typed in a link for Facebook. Once presented with the familiar blue marquee, typed in a name and hit the Enter key. Several options returned. He scanned them and followed one of the links. A number of pictures, despite a privacy setting on the profile. Pictures of coy poses for the camera, pouting with shades and fresh lipstick. Grinning over a cocktail while flanked by several other girls. Kieran studied the picture, focusing on one girl as he slowed the swivelling of his chair. Following the tagging of the face, he clicked on another profile. Read the small print and blinked, as though waking to bright light.

This is where bottling things up inside gets you.

Really. That's where you're going with this? Sneered at the screen.

Oblivious, the picture on-screen maintained the same carefree smile.

Really.

Pushing away from his computer, he got his feet and left the room, the swivel chair slowly rotating to a stop in his absence.

Darkness. Certainly by human standards.

By his standards, it would have to do.

Between pools of dull yellow light cast by streetlamps, the fox slunk alongside parked cars where possible, keeping close to the shadows and low to the ground. The smell of tarmac, the warm and oily scent of vehicle engines, some a shade warmer than others. Scents of refuse and possible food on the wind from up ahead.

Pickings were scarce but the fox had a job to do. This far from the den and with little food for the cubs meant the night's work would not be easy. The only consolation was that there were several hours of darkness yet.

He slunk forward into a crouch and waited, ears twitching. The drone came from his right and moments later, dipped headlights marked the passage of a car as it cruised through the crossroads. Not knowing the driver really couldn't give a shit about anything except getting home from a long night with a wasteman, the fox waited until the vehicle changed course to his left and moved out of sight. Then he trotted across the road and slunk into the shadow below the nearest car. Food: the scent of human scraps. Greasy rice and rich cooked meat, which was no less than a banquet compared to worms, spiders, and the occasional mouse. He inched forward from under the car and trotted along the pavement. The scent came through clear as a bell, and strong. There had to be a lot of food left for the taking.

He stopped, and tensed.

A new scent drifted to him on the wind, beyond the scent of food. A scent new to the neighbourhood, a nocturnal scent that had surfaced more than once before tonight.

The fox lifted his nose in the air, turning his muzzle this way and that. Still up ahead, but getting stronger by the moment. It smelled like a human, yet it also smelled like a... a dog. No, not dog. Something similar, but more wild. Regardless of what threats the night held in store, the food ahead was simply a commodity too scarce to pass up.

He scanned the street ahead. A narrow vista of darkened houses and parked cars stretching into the distance, along with the lampposts and telephone poles that punctuated the pavement. Still, the smell of food drifted from up ahead, rich and inviting. Another car cruised across the junction behind the fox, the beams cast from dipped headlights gliding through the darkness. Silence returned.

Too quiet.

The fox tensed, nose and ears twitching as its muzzle waved to and fro.

The scent blew across the fox from his left side, much closer than when it was up ahead of him, and at this range, the computation of risk took seconds: large animal, smell of human. Smell of dog, smell of not-dog. Turning away from padded footfalls, the fox bolted.

A cadence of paws *tha-dumped* behind it, closing the distance before a second of silence and a shadow overhead. Jaws clamped down over the fox's head, breaking the neck in the process.

Now the red-furred corpse hung limply from the predator's jaws as the hunter scanned the area, recovering its bearings. Blood leaked into its mouth from the fox's neck, and the hunter chuffed in disgust. This was vermin; not even an appetiser, but it would serve a purpose.

Bait.

For bigger prey.

Soon.

Jordan's Muesli, Alice decided, looked like currants mixed in with wood shavings: something she was pretty sure she had heard Chris Tarrant say long before *Who Wants To Be A Millionaire* was conceived. Jordan's may have been an acquired taste, but Alice was wary of caving to regular fry-ups. Muesli, fresh fruit, low-fat yoghurt and those kinds of things were the way to go now. She wolfed down the rest without tasting it and took a bite of her apple, eyelids shut against a glare of contempt. What kind of stupid name was Granny Smith for an apple, anyhow? The thing was vile: bitter as anything.

Footsteps approached in the hallway and Naomi leaned through the doorway, the black barista shirt and trousers in place. "I'm heading out now. See you later?"

"Okay, see you later."

Alice returned to her breakfast as Naomi left, pulling the door in behind her, footsteps retreating to the opening of the front door. Alice looked up at the wall clock, noting she still had a good ten minutes before she needed to head out. She returned her gaze to the apple, the skin around the bite green and shiny. The thing looked more like the skin of a… a frog or something. How Naomi could stomach these things was beyond her.

Alice frowned. She had heard Naomi leave the room, but…

She got to her feet and went out into the hallway, saw Naomi from behind, framed in the doorway. Naomi looked back over her shoulder. Her lips parted as though she were about to speak, then thought better of it.

"What's going on?"

Naomi turned away. "Come and look."

Alice drew up behind Naomi, and peered over her shoulder. "Oh, my God," she whispered.

At the top of the path lay a headless body of a dead fox, the stump of a neck upright against the front step, the air ferric. Blood stained the ground around the animal as well as the torn fur of the fox's chest. Several flies crawled across the corpse in seemingly random paths.

"Oh, my… God."

"I know."

"What the fuck happened?" she asked, breathless.

Naomi shook her head. "No idea. I know we had one or two foxes in the area—case in point," she said, gesturing at the mess in front of her, "but nothing else apart from that. Whatever dogs we have in the area would be walked by their owners, and no doubt back in their houses at night."

Alice swallowed and leaned harder against the wall, trying to keep herself calm and focused. "Do you think somebody did it? Trying to send a message, maybe?"

Naomi turned back to face her. "Who? And why?"

This close to the body, the scent of blood was cloying, an iron tang in the air. Alice was grateful for the distraction and hoped it wouldn't look that way. "You know, because of…" She tailed off, letting the insinuation sink in.

Naomi gave a wan smile. "A dead fox seems an odd way to go about it, doesn't it?" She took Alice's hand in her own and gave it a squeeze. "Go on, get out of here. You don't wanna be late—new job and all."

"What about you?"

"Don't worry about it," she said, patting Alice on the shoulder. "Go."

Alice ducked back inside to get her things and gave Naomi an air-kiss on the way out, tiptoeing over the fox as she left. More flies had joined the party, with one or two circling the neck and chest from time to time. At least if you were a fly, your morning would be off to a good start.

"That was alright," Kazu said, grinning up at the ceiling. He turned his head to look at Naomi in the darkness. She wondered if he knew that she would be gasping a lot more than she let on. He never failed to tire her out.

She snuggled into him, savouring the leanness of his body, the salty scent of sweat on his skin; hers, too. Sex wasn't meant to be clean and tidy. Moment by moment, her eyes adjusted to the gloom and picked out the room's features, from the duvet rumpled beyond her hips to the dresser at the far end of the room. The dumbbells on the floor. The suit hanging on the open door of the wardrobe.

Naomi nipped at his neck, felt his body tense. A smile curving her lips, she nipped at him again, brushing her lips against the skin.

"Hey, come on, stop it," he said, chuckling as he drew an arm around her shoulders. The grip pulled her in tight and she squealed in excitement.

"Sissy," she teased, poking him in the rib. "Who's a sissy?"

Another squeeze.

"Okay, okay, not you, not you!" she said, laughing.

She purred and nuzzled his nose, ending with lingering kisses. At last, she pulled back and rested her head on his chest.

"Better now?"

She nodded. "A lot better." She sighed in contentment. "I needed this."

Kazu chuckled. "It must be bad if you're saying it out loud. Tell me what's been going on. Is Alice giving you trouble?"

She pressed her head into him, enjoying the reverberation of his speech through his chest. "No, no trouble, nothing like that. We found a headless fox on our doorstep yesterday morning." She felt, more than heard, him look at her.

"Really?"

"Yeah. Blood and flies and everything. A real mess."

"Were you scared?"

"Scared?" She thought back to the mangled mess

of the previous morning. The scent of iron from the little corpse now reminded her of something in an abattoir. "No, not scared, no. But I did think that someone did something deliberately to get at Alice."

"What, because of her past?"

"Mmm-hmmm."

"What does Alice think?"

Naomi's mouth pulled into a grim line. "She thinks the same. I can't say I blame her either."

His lips trailed across her scalp, cascading hair into her eyes. He nuzzled it aside and kissed her on the forehead. "What do you think?"

"Honestly?" She chose her words carefully. "I think it's possible. Either that or there's something else prowling the neighbourhood at night, and apart from somebody's dog, I can't think of anything that would prey on a fox."

His hand on her shoulder now, warm and insistent. Naomi followed his direction and drew back to look at him. Even lying against the pillow, his hair remained upright and spiky. "You need to be careful," he said softly.

"Oh, don't worry, I'm going to be."

Reading paperbacks was nothing new for Alice, having read a number of them in prison. What was different was the sheer comfort that came from a night of quiet; curled up barefoot on one of the armchairs in the lounge, the cushion plush underneath her, and the comfort of the darkness outside. The nearby streetlight barely melted the gloom, but the single floor-standing lamp angled low at the floor provided just enough light to read by. The irony in enjoying isolation after having it enforced upon her over the last couple of years wasn't lost on Alice. Here, the setting was more agreeable—much more. From the occasional rumble of a vehicle cruising by in the darkness, to slow footsteps on the pavement, or the creak and muffled thump of movement from the upstairs flat, Alice stifled a grin. Naomi had expressed surprise on asking what Alice wanted, and hearing 'a good book would be enough.' Naomi didn't argue the point any more. Alice may have brought money into the flat, but after days apart, Kazu proved to be a more desirable proposition.

Alice pressed her face against the wall of the armchair and turned her attention back to her book. Three chapters into *Juicy Is What They Call Me* and she could already predict what would happen and who it would happen to. She gave a little chuckle of realisation and looked up from her book in a *whew* moment. Still, not a bad book at all.

Huh?

The man outside stood with his hands in his pockets as he scanned the upper floor of the house, craning his neck. From this angle, with his chin up, she could see a trimmed beard of stubble. Though buttoned, his shirt would flutter a little now and then, as would the collar.

Alice held her breath, as well as her movement.

The man's gaze trailed down the house to the front door with the slowness of honey pouring from a spoon. One corner of his mouth lifted in a smile, his gaze half-lidded. His eyebrows lifted in amusement.

Kieran?

Still maintaining the same beatific smile, he gave a little shrug.

Alice eased one hand off her book and braced it against the chair arm, her eyes never leaving Kieran's face.

He opened his mouth as if to speak, before heading to the front door, disappearing from view. The doorbell rang a moment later. Although it came as no surprise, Alice flinched anyway. Given the previous exchange between them, Alice hadn't expected to hear from Kieran again. Still, his behaviour did seem out of character, so maybe he was here to apologise after all. It was kind of late in the day though.

The doorbell rang again.

Alice slid off the chair and headed to the front door, opening it enough to bridge the gap with her body.

"Hey," Kieran said, gaze half-lidded against the night air. "I'm probably not one of your favourite people right now, but I figured I might owe you an apology. You already put yourself out there, so now

I guess it's my turn." He craned his neck as if peering behind her. "Can I come in? Naomi said it should be okay."

Alice stepped back from the door as Kieran let himself, gently shutting the door behind him. Arms folded, Alice made her way back to the lounge, seating herself in the chair nearest the door. Kieran entered soon after, taking the far seat by the window, fingers laced together in his lap, legs crossed at the ankles.

"Okay." Alice shrugged her shoulders in prompt. "I'm listening."

Kieran nodded. "I guess that means I should talk. So. I know I had hoped to start afresh, but that didn't quite go according to plan." Fingers still laced, he parted his thumbs. "You threw a drink in my face. I threw an apology back in yours. It doesn't look like either of us are good at this."

"No, it doesn't."

Kieran sat forward, uncrossing his legs. "Alice? I'm sorry."

There it was. Alice didn't think she would hear it or deserve to hear it, but there it was, out in the open. Pride stopped Alice from making a full-blown apology (and she *had* spent two years in prison as a big apology), so she settled for a subdued 'thank you.'

Kieran clapped a hand on his thigh. "Well. I'm glad that's over with, at least," he said, prompting a rueful smile from Alice. "Did you have any idea what I was coming here for?"

"I didn't, no," Alice said, shifting in the chair. "I wasn't even sure it was you at first, and then when I saw it was? I don't know, I was just caught completely off guard."

"I can imagine. I mean, that rape accusation from way back caught *me* off guard. I mean, rape?" His gaze lingered on her. A corner of his mouth lifted in that half-smile again; the expression of a card sharp about to reveal the ace in the hole. "What would you do if I *was* here to rape you?"

What?

Rather than respond, Kieran simply sat there, waiting.

Alarm pricked at her gut, with an almost-physical sensation of being needled.

"I'll tell you one thing," he said, holding up a forefinger. "Naomi doesn't know I'm here."

So how did *Kieran* know?

Oh, no.

Alice scrambled to her feet and darted for the door.

Something bulky and unyielding caught her in the back, flooring her and whooshing the air from her lungs in the process. A panicked backward glance revealed an upturned armchair on her leg—and Kieran still on the *other side of the room.*

W-w-what?!

"How about that?" Faint surprise lilted Kieran's voice. "That was a good shot."

Alice stretched a hand to the door, panting, and felt the weight of the armchair give a little. Working on freeing her leg, she rocked sideways, the chair shifting on top—

"Alice?" came Kieran's voice from across the room. "Look at me."

Alice ground her teeth and swallowed. The door was close, the doorknob was close, and the chair wasn't so heavy. She turned to look at him.

He stood across the room, silhouetted against the night outside the window.

"What…?" On second thought, no. No, she did *not* want to know what he fucking wanted, not at all, and her heart hammered in her chest, making it hard to think clearly.

"Wait a minute," he said.

And dropped to his knees.

Alice's gut tightened. She had heard stories of rape before—too many for her liking. The strongest, most outgoing and confident women could still be victims. Advice ranged from fighting back to not fighting back at all, and right now, she had no idea what the best course of action would be.

He crawled closer, the dragging of his knees on carpet a dreadful harbinger of what might come. He came to a stop less than a yard away, his eyes on hers.

"Did you get my message?"

What? What the…? "Your message?"

"No?" He shook his head slowly, a trace of a

smile still in place. "I guess your flatmate cleans up after you. But that's not why I'm here. So here's the key question. Do you know why I'm here?"

Alice's mind raced. She could guess the answer, yeah, *guess*, but a wrong answer could go badly for her and at least if she said she didn't know, it would be truthful and maybe it...

She shook her head.

His gaze slid over her. "Did you think that I would rape you?"

Her gut tightened, her pulse thudding harder.

"Did you? Tell the truth now. There's no right or wrong answer here."

Alice gave a slow nod, her eyes wide. Kieran gave that half-smile again, and Alice felt her heartbeat lurch.

"You know," Kieran said. "You probably would think that. After all, it's that very stupid lie you told that brought us here in the first place. That's what you get for crying wolf: a whole lot of trouble. Never mind that you drag my name through the mud." His nostrils flared, etching creases alongside his nose, contempt visible in the tightness of his mouth. "But then, when I decide to let bygones be bygones and extend you an olive branch, you throw it back in my face. Not once, but twice." He breathed a sigh of irritation.

"So," he said. "This is where we get to what *I* want. Are you listening?" He leaned in closer, and Alice could smell a faint tang of soap under the laundered fabric of his shirt. "Because you'd better be. If you so much as scream, if you look away for even a moment? I will *end* you," he said through gritted teeth. "Right here and now."

Alice nodded weakly.

"Good." He nodded to himself, his mouth a grim line. "Just remember this: no one will believe you."

Kieran grunted, grimacing as though taking the force of a blow. From somewhere behind him, Alice heard something pop, like the crack of a knuckle. Then again. Alice peered sideways at him, trying to see where...

Oh.

Skin on the back of Kieran's hands began to ripple and pulsate: slow tidal waves of flesh cascading up his forearms. The fingers that he dug into the carpet began to shorten while the palms of his hands began to lengthen. A thin line of hairs oozed from the backs of his fingers and hands. She looked back to his face, and gasped. His forehead pulsed and lowered into a frown, as his jaws pushed out of his face in a... *muzzle* while his ears had moved nearer the top of his head and grown pointed. Each gasp or grunt grew deeper than the last. The fabric of his shirt grew tight around the shoulders and back until the shirt tore, the sound cutting through the silence with harsh clarity. Hair crawled from the sweat-sheened skin, and as Kieran's head hung lower, Alice could see his shoulder blades lengthen, pulling the ruined shirt apart even further. Still the snaps like the cracking of knuckles continued, from Kieran's face, to his body, his legs: everywhere. A harsher sound now, as shoe leather stretched and tore, and Kieran groaned in response.

Tears of fright leaked from her eyes and Alice sobbed, digging her fingers into the carpet.

I will end you.

Oh no, oh no, oh no, oh no.

By now, Kieran's nose had cleft in the middle, darkening, and as he coughed a growl, more hair began to crawl from his pores.

Alice's tears ran freely now.

The last shred of shirt, complete with the collar, hung over one of the animal's shoulders.

The animal swung its head to look over its shoulder, before leaning sideways, letting the shirt slide to the floor. It returned its gaze to Alice, and she whimpered louder. One word filled her mind, smothering rational thought and normalcy.

Wolf.

Rumbling now: reverberation through the floor. Through the tears Alice gaped, and only when it grew louder and she saw the muzzle wrinkle back, fangs framing the mouth in pink gums, did she place the sound.

The animal growled louder, the fur bristling now.

Alice bit her lip and hitched a sob. Her bladder suddenly felt heavy.

Bracing her hands against the carpet, she heaved

her foot out from under the armchair, toppling it over with a thud. Her hand slapping itself over the doorknob, she yanked the door open and dashed from the room. Behind her, weight slammed the door shut a fraction of a second later.

Alice whirled back toward the door and pulled it in with both hands as a growl rang out from the other side, loud enough that she felt the vibration of it through the doorknob.

Ohshitohshitohshitohshit...

Inside the room on the other side of the door, the animal waited.

It raised its muzzle to the doorknob and inhaled. Moisturiser. Skin. Sweat. *Fear.*

A growl of pleasure.

It backed away. To do so was a rebellion against its nature, but food wasn't the primary aim of this evening.

Fear was.

The animal surveyed the room, from the overturned furniture to the window. In much the same way that a person may feel more businesslike when wearing a suit, so the animal felt more lupine in a predatory form, and, as such, to maintain a human control and perspective took some effort.

Alice.

A snarl of contempt, and then the animal lifted its leg and sprayed an arc of urine onto the sofa and carpet, before bounding through the window in a shower of glass and into the night.

On the other side of the door, Alice heard the thump of paws and the breaking of the window.

Then silence.

She still held the doorknob in both hands, leaning back.

Fatigue began to set in.

Soon she collapsed to the floor and her sweat-slicked palms slid over the doorknob, which slipped from her grasp. The door swung in a little and she gasped, screwing her eyes shut.

The echo of night sounded from the other side of the door. And it was there in the stillness, in the aftermath, that the questions began to crowd in on her.

I will end you.

But he hadn't. Why?

Why? Because he wanted her to suffer—*that* was why.

He? *It.*

IT. That.

Like many people, Alice liked the occasional horror film, and while the likes of *The Texas Chainsaw Massacre* or *Paranormal Activity* had given her a jump scare or two, they had never given her a sleepless night. For what she had just seen, her first thought was 'dog,' but no—Kieran didn't turn into a dog.

Werewolf.

The animal was simply too big. Savage.

Werewolf.

The problem went deeper than that, much deeper.

No one will believe you.

"Oh, God," she whispered. "Oh, God, oh, God, oh, God."

And she sat there, her knees drawn up to her chest and her arms wrapped around her shins like a frightened child, until she mustered enough courage to head back into that room and retrieve her phone.

PART 2

BLUE LIGHTS CONTINUED to strobe the darkness as the last officer left and Naomi, still a little bleary-eyed, thanked him for his timely response before seeing him out. As the front door closed, Naomi came back into the room and, casting a cursory glance at Alice, made her way to the broken window and watched as the police car pulled away into the night. Across the street and two doors down, an upstairs bedroom showcased a silhouette behind a net curtain, which disappeared minutes later. Naomi exhaled a sigh through her nose before turning away from the window and raising her eyebrows in a gesture of feigned nonchalance. She folded her arms, the sleeves of the basketball jersey she wore resting on her forearms.

Alice felt the weight of her gaze like a hand on her shoulder. "Thank you."

"That's okay," Naomi replied, her voice neutral.

"I do live here, after all. What was I supposed to do?"

Alice shrugged. "You could've stayed curled up in bed with Kazu."

"Oh, no. That would have been too easy." She gave a wry chuckle. "I'll make it up to him, for which I know he'll be eternally grateful."

Naomi crossed the room to sit beside Alice on the dry part of the sofa. "Fucking drunks," she muttered as she regarded the wetness staining the carpet. "It stinks like a zoo in here."

Wary, Alice tensed and gave a sidelong glance.

Moments passed in excruciating silence, until Alice found she could start to relax. With the jagged hole in the window barely boarded up and the ambient sounds drifting in from outside, the night brought goose bumps up on her bare arms.

"So," Naomi said. "Why don't you tell me what really happened?"

Alice turned to look at Naomi. The woman still held a bleary-eyed look, but the set of her jaw said that, interrupted sleep or not, tea and sympathy were still a way away.

"I told you," Alice said. "Some drunk guys broke in."

Naomi licked her lips. "Yes, I know that's what you told me. I know that's what you told the officers because I was there when it happened. But what you're not telling is what *really* happened. So let's try again. What really happened?"

I will end you.

Alice looked down at her hands clasped in her lap. At least right now, her hands felt smooth—wonderfully so. Funny how something so nightmarish could be... good for the skin. Was it really? Did that even make sense? She held her hands together, and looked up across the room, noting Naomi out the corner of her eye, still posed waiting for a response.

"Alice, don't play stupid, I'm still waiting. I don't have all night."

No one will believe you. Alice had seen it and *she* barely believed it. At least she made sure to bin the tattered clothing before anyone else got to the scene of the crime anyway.

She clasped her hands tighter. "I'm..." She wrung her hands in her lap, thinking how best to put it into words, how best to articulate it without sounding as if she were completely crazy. "I'm honestly not sure what happened." At least that was true.

A pause, followed by a whoosh of breath. "Okay. Was it Rebecca?"

"What?" Alice whirled on her friend, still seeing the same sleepy-eyed look. "Rebecca? Seriously?"

"Okay, was it Kieran?"

Caught off-guard, Alice sat there, mentally rummaging for a suitable answer and not finding any. Not such a good liar after all.

Naomi held her cheek on her fist, her forefinger

against her temple. "Why am I not surprised? Hmmm?"

Right now, Alice felt nothing but stupidity: a chattering child shamed into silence by the scolding of an adult.

"Dare I even ask what Kieran wants with you? Because I seem to remember the last time you mentioned his name, you had not only insulted him, but you were about to rub salt into the wound—despite me warning you against it."

No words would come. The truth was too outlandish to reveal. Worse was the knowledge that somewhere in this one-sided discussion, the 'I told you so' would rear up and strike. Along with shame and embarrassment.

"Look," Naomi said. "I agreed to help you get back on your feet, but it doesn't look like you're helping yourself or doing yourself any favours, you know?" Her shoulders lifted a little. "So as we discussed when you first moved in here, I'm going to ask you to move out."

Her gaze still on the wall opposite, Alice's stomach tightened as though she were about to take a punch to the gut.

"The best thing I can suggest for now is that we both get a good night's sleep, and then we can get sorted out in the morning."

OH, no. Alice was hardly safe *at the house*, so what chance did she have out there? Her voice barely made it above a whisper. "You can't."

Naomi scoffed. "You seem to be forgetting something," she said, her voice soft. "When you were released, I offered to take you in. I can imagine there were those who would say no, but I figured I would look past that, since we all have lives to live. Don't forget that I'm under no obligation to you—you, however, who would stay in my home, are. Now maybe against my better judgement, I shouldn't have made that call."

At this point, Alice turned to Naomi, and saw the other woman sitting up straight, the haze of sleep cleared from her eyes.

"I don't deny prison may have been rough on you, but neither do I doubt that it was a wake-up call. No, I don't want to know what happened with Kieran way back when. What I *do* know is that when someone is released from prison, it should be a chance to move forward and learn from past mistakes. One run-in with Kieran since may be accidental, yeah, but two is just plain careless. More importantly, it shows that you're still making bad choices, and that you can't *own up* to the fact that you're making bad choices, and frankly, I don't want your bad choices spilling over onto me. I think I'm being quite reasonable, all things considered.

"Where's your phone?" she asked, jerking her chin at Alice.

"It's here. Why?"

"Because you're going to need it. Get a good night's sleep. First thing in the morning, you're moving out. I'll even help."

"What?" Her voice sounded timid in her ears.

"You're leaving in the morning."

Seeing the transformation up close was bad enough, being close enough to see the skin of Kieran's mouth stretch to accommodate a muzzle of fangs. In the quiet of the aftermath and the departure of the police, there was a sense of safety —relative safety, at least. But to leave now? Alice didn't doubt that if Kieran could do what he just did, he could find her, *and he wasn't even human now! How could any human being do what Kieran just did?* She gasped, inhaled saliva and coughed, her pulse accelerating.

Naomi sat through it unruffled.

"I can't."

"You can," Naomi said, her voice weary. "You will." And with that, she left the room.

Later, Alice pushed to her feet, her panties clinging with cold wetness, and left the room. As she pulled the door closed, the memory of trying to hold the door in against Kieran came back to her in an almost tangible reference: the pressure of her grip pressing the doorknob into her palms. The best course of action now, she decided, was to get what little sleep she could before getting her stuff together. Right now, a clean pair of panties was the first port of call.

A knock sounded at the front door, at which Naomi cast a blank look at Alice. "Have you got everything?"

"Not a whole lot to get, is there?" Alice said, her tone hard. She clenched her jaw, remembering Naomi's words from the previous night. "Yeah. I've got everything, thanks."

"Good." Cordial conversation now, business-like and nothing more. "Let me see you off."

"Oh no, you don't have to."

"Don't worry about it, it's no trouble."

Alice shouldered her holdall and wheeled her suitcase out behind her in her left hand. The movement was awkward with the wheels of the case bumping against the skirting board. Naomi held the door open for her.

Richard stood just beyond the front step, the collar of his polo shirt sharp as if it were over-ironed, his hair an artfully shaggy mess. "Morning, ladies."

"Hi, morning." Alice rested a hand on Richard's cheek. "Thanks for helping out on such short notice."

He gave a nod. "Ahhh, it's no trouble, honestly." He gestured behind him to the gate. "Shall we?"

Well, nobody else would, she though bitterly. All the other calls made were met with apologies (or in one case, a text) in varying degrees of conviction.

Alice joined him beyond the front step, scanning the street. Naomi watched her, unblinking, before her gaze returned to Richard. As Alice headed through the gate, Richard gave Naomi a nod. Her only response was a clouding of her gaze, as whatever trace of a smile there may have been disappeared. Solemn now, Richard nodded in return. Joining Alice outside the gate, he loaded her bags into his car and, his failed attempts at conversation notwithstanding, drove them a laboured path in slow traffic and busy streets until reaching a back street in Kennington. Richard helped Alice out with her bags and led her around to the main road where late morning had brought a glut of pedestrians, a steady flow of traffic, and from somewhere across the street, a soulful rendition of Bob Marley's "Jammin'. Alice tracked the singing to a lanky Rastafarian whose dreadlocks were greying visibly from a distance.

"He's jammin', all right," Richard said as they picked a path through pedestrians. They walked a little further until they came to a launderette. Richard fished a key from his pocket and slid it into the door adjacent to the launderette's doorway. "Just up here," he said, taking the suitcase from her. "Go on up."

Alice complied. Darker and cooler than outside, the stairway smelled a little musty, and the wood of the stairs creaked under her weight. Something in her gait must have revealed her apprehension, as Richard said, "Don't worry, the stairs are good. Just a little further." Once on the landing, Alice came to a varnished door of unpainted wood. Richard followed behind her and, hip-checking her aside, unlocked the door, finishing with a flourish. "Go right in."

Although small, the flat appeared spacious with a two-seater sofa along one wall and two table chairs flanking it at opposite ends of the room. Daylight flooded in from the windows on the right hand side, double glazing muting the sounds outside from the main road. Alice nodded in approval and made her way to the next room, the slow pace of her boots the only sound. The kitchen was small and clean (the worktops were spotless, she noticed), the bathroom similarly clean. A surreptitious peek under the flap of the kitchen bin revealed the remnants of a stale takeaway curry, along with some orange peel. She browsed the cupboards, noting a bare assortment of condiments, along with a few Pot Noodles. Footsteps sounded behind her, and she looked back at Richard, who lifted his gaze from her waist to eye level.

"Are you hungry?" he asked. "It's a little early for lunch, maybe, but I threw a salad together. Nothing too fancy, just some grilled chicken with a little pasta, some mixed greens…" He tailed off.

"A salad?" she asked, incredulous. Richard's smile flashed a pang of embarrassment and Alice chided herself, her eyes closed as she shook her head. "No, thank you. That's lovely, but no. Right now, a coffee would be great."

"Sure. You can make yourself comfortable in the bedroom or the lounge. Coffee won't be too long."

"You're sweet," she said, and turned on her heel, heading to the last room. The bedroom itself was compact, with the bed taking up most of the far wall. The dresser, clustered with bottles of aftershave and eau de toilette, stood along the next wall, while a widescreen TV stood at the other end of the room. Below the TV sat a neat stack of Auto Trader magazines. Alice nodded in approval and made her way into the kitchen, where Richard held an upturned cup over the sink, the scent of coffee in the air.

"Sorry," he said, on seeing her at the doorway. "I made the coffee first without asking how you like it."

Her gaze half-lidded, she gave a shake of her head, a smile playing on her lips. "One sugar and a splash of milk, thanks."

Richard followed the instructions and handed the cup to her, clasping its sides as though warming his hands. Alice took it gratefully, lowering her head for a sip as Richard gave a wince, fingers clenching for a moment.

"Mmmm," she said. "Good coffee, thank you. You're not having one?"

"No. I have coffee every now and then, but I'm more an apple juice man, me."

They headed back to the lounge where Alice seated herself on the chair facing the window. Richard cocked his head at her, before seating himself nearby at the edge of the sofa.

"The bed's yours as long as you want it," he said, hands spread wide in supplication. "I'll take the sofa. Just as long as you get yourself back on your feet, okay?"

"You're sure?" she asked, peering at him over her coffee cup.

"Sure, I'm sure. Let's get you straightened out first."

"Thank you."

They sat in silence for a while as Alice sipped her coffee.

"So: you and Naomi."

Alice tensed.

"What exactly happened between you two? I mean, I know it's none of my business, but I may be able to help or something."

Alice exhaled a sigh under the guise of blowing on her coffee; the drink was hot to start with, but perfectly fine now. "Look, Rich. I know you mean well, but right now, I just want to put it behind me." She smoothed her hair away from her neck, Richard following it with his gaze. "She... reminded me that I should be moving forward and learning from mistakes, so that's what I'm trying to do. I want to leave those bad choices in the past."

"Okay. So how does that relate to the break-in yesterday? Is that as a result of a bad choice or something?"

I will end you.

She lowered her eyes, taking a moment to collect herself. "No," she said. "No, not a bad choice, but I guess we were getting under each other's feet too often. Don't get me wrong," she said quickly, "I'm grateful that she took me in when she did. But now?" She gave a wan smile. "Maybe our honeymoon period as flatmates is over."

Richard gave a smile of sympathy, and Alice smiled with him as she weighed him up. He sat forward at the edge of the sofa. Elbows on his knees his hands dangling, his eyes locked on hers in earnest. He was a sweet guy.

"I'm not ready for a new... flatmate yet," she said. "But..." Inside, the façade of her smile cracked. What did that leave—gazing at the floor? Yeah, sure.

I will end you.

Nothing could have prepared her for that.

Her voice was soft. "Sometimes these things happen when you least expect them, right?"

Richard pointed a finger in affirmation and clicked his tongue. "They do indeed. So," he said, his tone lifting. "What do you want to do now? Sleep, maybe?"

Sleep? She let the thought sink in. Sure, she managed to grab a couple of hours or so yesterday night, but that hadn't been the most restful sleep. The memory of Kieran in the flat, having shifted from human to something clearly *not* human, rose to the fore. At least in the bright light of day, in a humdrum setting with Richard, it felt like life might have a chance at normalcy again.

"Go for it," he said. "I have an errand to run a little later. I'm usually in and out. Besides, I'm thinking you could probably use some time and space to take a load off."

Alice let those words sink, his expression earnest. As a guard for London Underground who liked pulling overtime, Richard had more than the day job to keep him busy. The vein in his neck pulsed, distracting her for a moment. "Thank you."

He waved it off before shooing her out, where she headed to the bedroom and rummaged through her holdall, pulling out a fresh t-shirt. A quick change later and she lay on top of the bed, the duvet cover cool beneath her. Introspection returned.

Werewolf.

The idea sounded surreal and had Alice not seen it herself, she wouldn't have believed it, which led her to the questions of *when* and *how?* While at least two years had passed since she had seen Kieran, he was still most likely a creature (and here, Alice cringed at the mental use of the word)… a creature of habit. During their relationship, they both held down jobs that were more or less nine to five, which left them evenings for dinner dates, catching a film here and there, or individual interests. As for the sex, sure, it was good, but it was just with one guy, so in entertaining more than one prospect, Alice ensured she kept her options open. Unlike Kieran, Alice didn't want anything serious. Or so she thought. When Kieran broke off the relationship, Alice's insecurities and impulsive nature drove her to lash out and accuse him of something despicable, ultimately landing her in jail for two years. Plenty of time for Kieran to… change.

From having dated him, slept in his bed and fucked him, there were no indicators she could think of back then that would point to his duality: no excess body hair, craving undercooked meat or any clichés like that. So somehow, in that time, Kieran had changed. Bitten, maybe? But then, the 'how' was truly a moot point.

Alice thrust her head back into the pillow, savouring the thickness of it; enough thickness to keep her head elevated. Much better than at Naomi's place, where everything for the bed had to be soft: including the mattress. Alice laced her fingers behind her head, stifling a yawn as she looked to the window. With this side of the flat receiving western exposure, she wouldn't have to worry about the heat during the afternoon. Not too much, she hoped.

Minutes later, Alice fell asleep, with all thoughts of Kieran momentarily forgotten.

"Fumi, are you free to give this lady a hand?"

Fumi turned and approached the woman. "Hey,

how can I help?" she asked, her smile lighting her eyes. The customer, slim and pony-tailed with an earring in her nose, responded in kind. Neither of them acknowledged Alice.

Only two days had passed since she had moved out of Naomi's flat, and already Alice felt she had adapted to the new routine well. Richard wasn't the most accomplished cook: his pasta was plain apart from some salt and pepper, but somehow the grilled chicken was flavoursome. His fried breakfasts were better. Alice took it upon herself to cook more, read more: anything more to keep herself busy and keep her mind active. She'd have to do something about a social life too: all work and no play made Jill a dull girl.

She looked over at Fumilola, now in full swing with the customer, leaning in close and hanging on the customer's every word, smiling where appropriate and all the while with her back turned to Alice, so she wouldn't have to see her at all.

Alice lowered her hand out of sight beneath the counter and clenched her fist. Her nails bit into her palm.

Next to her, the slanted tray of lipsticks looked a little sparse, and she pulled them forward in their rows, making the racks look as full as possible to the casual observer. Ahead of her, a teenage boy walked through the crowd with his girlfriend and cast Alice a lingering look. She watched him pass, the boy now looking over his shoulder as he disappeared into the crowd. *Typical,* she thought. Never mind that the fact that—

"Excuse me, but how much is this one?"

Alice turned, her eyes widening. Around her, the crowd continued to drift through the store.

Kieran made his way to the counter from her far right, his stubble beard immaculate. Another long sleeve shirt, a similar cut and pattern to the one he wore when he… he…

I will end you.

"This one here," he said, pointing at a lipstick in the rack. "How much is this one? Please?"

Alice pressed her palms against the sides of the glass case in front of her, rather than on top. "What do you want?" Her legs began to tremble.

"Errr, I told you what I want," he said. "That one." He pointed at the trays.

She gave a slow nod, willing herself to stay calm. "W-w-would you show me exactly which one, please?" Her voice wavered, and she gritted her teeth because of it.

His finger swept in a slow arc away from the shelves and came to rest pointing at her. "This one," he said. "This is the one I want. Right here."

Alice forced herself to look him in the eye. He eyed her from across the counter, shoppers behind him drifting by, some even brushing past, yet his gaze remained unflinching.

"What do you want?"

Kieran feigned ambivalence. "What do I want? I

just want to see how you're doing, that's all—after all, I'm sure the last couple of nights can't have been easy for you. Did you sleep okay?"

Her heart punched away in her chest and the longer she stood there, the more acutely aware she became of her pulse in her temples.

Kieran's brows lowered in a glare. "Because I sure as hell hope not," he said, his voice low and thick. "Do you know what? Some of it actually makes me kind of happy—that you're easy to read." His gaze narrowed as he drew his nose through the air, as though tracing a caress back and forth along her shoulder and neck. "I can tell that you're not eating so healthy. Sure, there's a lot of make up and perfume here in this department but that doesn't explain what's most likely the smell of eggs and bacon on you. Most likely comfort food, since I remember how you would get on a muesli and fruit kick any time you thought your midsection was giving way to a muffin top."

Alice flinched as though he'd raised a hand at her.

"*Now* I can smell something else beneath the Issey Miyake and Dove soap. Know what it is? *Fear.*" He gave a grim nod. "That's what I like the smell of. That's a good start."

Alice straightened her arms and pushed back from the counter, turning away as much as she dared. Fumi had long since finished with the lady that Alice had called her for, and was now busy with another customer. Carrie was also likewise engaged.

"This is good," Kieran said, patting the counter for emphasis. "No one to step in and save you, nothing left for you to do but run. I don't know why you moved away from Naomi anyhow; it seems like you had quite a good thing going there." He picked up a lipstick from the nearby rack and rolled it between his fingers, looking at the label on the base as he did so. "Maybe things just weren't working out for you."

"Kieran…" She bit her lip, struggling to find the words. "Why?" she asked weakly. "Why are you doing this?"

Kieran blinked. "Why? Why am I doing this? Errr, because I can?" He pointed the lipstick at her. "Because after what you did, I think you deserve it." With that, he put the lipstick back in its rack, fussing with the rows. "That's why. Is that enough reason for you?"

Kieran craned his neck and Alice tensed. His gaze bore into her. Amid the hubbub of the department, a growl rumbled in his chest and he bared his teeth in a grimace at her. Full lips, somewhat dry, curled back as his canines lengthened. Alice stared in disbelief. Exhaling a gasp, Kieran's muzzle pushed an inch out of his face before halting in a cracking of bone, while his hands pushed harder at the counter. The muzzle now melted back into his face until laboured breathing was the only sign that anything had happened at all.

"I'm not done with you by a long shot, Miss Morecambe, so you be sure to keep looking over your shoulder." He patted the counter again, leaving tiny crescents of sweat where his fingertips touched the glass. "Downwind, Alice. That's where I'll be."

He turned and cut a path to the left, heading into the crowd and past the escalators by the main entrance. Alice's gaze flitted to and fro, from face to face, and all she saw were browsers and shoppers, but no spectators.

Down in the far reaches of the auditorium, more people were starting to file in. So far, the screen curtains were still closed, with orchestral scores from previous motion pictures piped through the theatre's speakers. Standard operating procedure.

Richard eased back in his seat, his elbow brushing Naomi's. The thing with the Vue cinema was, unlike the Odeon, it would accommodate taller people with plenty of legroom. He didn't have to worry about kicking someone else's leg and setting off an argument, or the whole passive-aggressive thing where you'd stretch—

"What are you grinning about?"

He turned to Naomi, saw her looking at him with an air of amusement.

"Nothing," he said. "Just enjoying the legroom. He cast a look at her feet and the abundance of space between them and the seat in front. "I guess

I'll just have to enjoy it for you."

"Yeah," she muttered, giving him a playful slap on his shoulder. "Why don't you do that?"

He reached for his Coke and took a sip, ice cubes giving a hollow knock against the inside of the container as he looked at the seats in front. Still not a whole lot of people coming in now, but then, *Batman v Superman* had been out in cinemas for a while. This time of day, when the city finished work, they'd go home to family or maybe hit a bar for a drink or two; but whatever they chose, BvS wouldn't be high on that list. Plus, from what Richard had heard, reviews weren't so favourable. Not that he would let that stop him. In comic fandom, you had to pick either Marvel or DC and since Marvel was now under the House Of Mouse, DC was the only way to go. He turned to Naomi.

"How are things between you and Alice?"

Naomi shrugged. "Fine. Why?"

Richard took another sip of his Coke before returning it to the holder of his chair arm. "Just wondered, that's all."

Naomi gave a wry chuckle. "It's not me you should be worrying about."

"Oh, really?" He shifted in his seat to face her.

"Richard, look," she said, shaking her head. "I know you might have a bit of a thing for her, and to be fair—"

"No, I don't."

"—and to be *fair*," she said, resting a hand on his

forearm, "I'm sure Alice knows it too. But the girl's trouble. You're a guy. I get it, you might see things differently, but she doesn't have a whole lot of respect for men. The girl doesn't have a whole lot of respect for *herself*."

Richard laid a hand on top of hers, enjoying the softness of her skin as her knuckles moved beneath his palm. "I think you're being a little hard on her. Sure, she's made mistakes, but then, so does everybody. You need to leave the past in the past and move on. That's what Alice is trying to do."

"You're sure about that?"

"Aren't you?"

What Naomi didn't want to do was argue, not with Richard. Superheroes weren't her thing, but she was grateful that he offered to pick up the bill and treat her to a film: partly because she could use the escapism. Not that she'd willingly admit it out loud. "She's impulsive, and she makes bad decisions because of it. Sometimes with men."

"Maybe she was a cocktease once upon a time," he said, "but even if she was, that doesn't mean she's the same person now. People can change. Remember, she only got out of prison a little while ago after how many years inside. This is already a rough time for her, so she's still adjusting. That's not gonna happen overnight."

Naomi sighed and shot him a look of resignation. "True." As someone whose last girlfriend *was* a habitual flirt (or cocktease, for less syllables), maybe Richard had the right perspective. *My God,* she thought, *he might have a point.*

Rocking her foot from side to side, Alice eased her heel into the other shoe, before standing to assess the pair in the nearest mirror. Celeste moved closer, while Office staff and other shoppers bustled around them.

"I like these, yeah," she said, nodding at the shoes on her feet. The vamp sat low enough to give the barest hint of toe cleavage; the shoes even brought out the tone in her calves. Pretty.

"You see?" Celeste said. "That's what I was saying. It's not another day at the office. You go with a nude patent and it's simple, yet classy. That's what you want for the big day."

Alice turned her back to the mirror and peered over her shoulder. Her calves looked good too, more shapely since she had returned to life outside. "You could be right, you know."

"You think?"

Of course Celeste was right. The girl couldn't cook for shit, which at least was *something* that Alice could do better. No, Celeste's area of expertise, one of them, was fashion. Case in point.

Grinning, Alice returned to the stool and slid the shoes off. "I'll take them," she said to the assistant that returned to her side, before making her way to the till and paying. Glossy bag in hand, Alice turned to Celeste. "Shall we?"

Outside of Office, Westfield in Shepherds Bush saw plenty of foot traffic at this time of the evening —those who would window shop or look at the attractions like the latest tech display plaza, or want to dine at one of the Southern Terrace restaurants before or after actually buying something from one of the stores. The past few days since Kieran's warning had seen Alice finally get the bridesmaid dress fitted, and return to a feeling of normalcy. Of course, you couldn't have the dress and no shoes, so, retail therapy aside, Alice enlisted Celeste to hang out and provide a second opinion when there were shoes to be bought. Two birds with one stone, as Celeste worked at a local NatWest.

"Do you want to hit Wagamama's or something?" Alice asked as they walked. "My treat."

"No, thank you. Japanese food isn't really my thing."

"So what's your thing, then? I hear there's a great Lebanese place nearby too. I'm not sure about the Italian place they got here, but they've got loads of other places. Or even a Nando's, if you want to go with the safe and really healthy option."

"Honestly," Celeste said, "it's not a problem. If anything, I wouldn't mind a biryani or something. It has been quite a while since I had some Indian food. I need to reacquaint myself with something spicy."

"Spicy?" Alice pondered her options. "There's the Cinnamon Kitchen, I think, which is only up at

Liverpool Street, so we're looking at a straight journey there, no changes. We've also got the Mintleaf, which comes highly recommended. I can't remember by who, or else I'd ask them for directions as well. Cinnamon Kitchen all right?"

No answer.

"I said," Alice said, turning, "we——"

Alice was alone.

An Indian couple strolled past, a wide-eyed toddler perched on the man's shoulders. Yards away in the milling crowd, a bearded hipster leaned against a pillar, scanning something on his smartphone.

A cursory glance of the shopping concourse gave nothing away. Nearby stores with eager staff approaching customers that drifted through the store, Celeste not among them. One staff member backed away from a woman eyeing a handbag on a display carousel, her attention not needed if the woman was just looking.

Alice whirled, her heart lurching in her chest. *Where….?*

She couldn't have turned away for more than a minute and in that time, Celeste had disappeared. Alice scanned her surroundings, from the line of shops on her left, the escalators, the centre concourse, the lift bay on the far side.

Where are you, where are you, where are you?

From here, she could see up onto the first floor, where a group of kids leaned over one side of the railing, peering down at ground level. Adults, standing taller, walked past them: one Indian man with his arm draped over his lady's shoulders as she caressed his dangling fingers. Back at ground level, a member of Westfield security in the blazer and trousers combo, armband clearly visible as he paced the length of the wall on the other side of the atrium.

No!

Kieran, some yards away, flashed her a grin and strolled toward her.

Bag forgotten, it slid from her hand as Alice turned and ran. Running footsteps closed the distance from her far right, alongside her and then ahead of her. A panicked turn to her left revealed a dead end with toilet alcoves on each side and a series of glass doors on her right. Alice sped toward one of them and raced out into the car park, slowing to a halt. Gleaming vehicles sat parked in rows, with a number of spaces vacant throughout the floor. A pedestrian crossing ran the length of the park under a ceiling lined with bright fluorescent tubes. One car, already pulling out of its parking space, cruised to the down ramp and out of sight.

Alice pivoted, looking behind her. The glass doors she'd raced out of remained closed, a receptionist at the desk further inside. On the other side of the foyer next to the escalators, an Indian couple sat, looking bored. Alice swallowed hard, and swung away, scanning the parking area, forcing herself to——

The parking area plunged into darkness, making Alice yelp as something thudded behind her to the far right with an electrical sizzle. A gasp came from up ahead at the far end of the sheltered walkway before the final sound of receding footsteps. What little light from the other side of the glass doors fell short of Alice, barely throwing light on the nearest cars and pillars. Within the foyer, the receptionist leaned forward over the counter, peering into the darkness. A black-suited man, a bronze badge on his lapel, marched over to her and rested one hand on the counter. A low and airy whistle came from Alice's far right; a human whistle, before melting into another note. The melody picked up speed until it resolved itself into the White Stripes' "Seven Nation Army."

Fuck off and fuck you, Alice thought with a grimace, heading into the darkness. As she moved, so did the whistling, keeping pace with her. Eyes now adjusting to the gloom, Alice picked out the silhouettes of vehicles and pillars as she moved deeper into the car park. Keeping low, she headed to a van parked at the far wall, the dull gleam of car windows and bodywork winking as she pressed on. Now close enough to touch the rear of the vehicle, she groped behind it for a crawlspace. Her fingertips, damp with sweat, dragged along the vehicle's bodywork. Was that sound too loud? She paused.

Nothing but the sound of her breathing.

Slowly turning her head, she watched the parking area. No movement as far as she could tell. No sound as far as she could tell. Nothing but stillness, and the faint smell of tyre rubber. No parking of vehicles, no footsteps, no snatches of conversation.

No whistling.

Alice bit her lip, trying to remember how long had passed since she heard him. The worst of it was that just because she couldn't locate him, that didn't mean he couldn't locate her. Especially if Kieran... wasn't Kieran anymore.

Ohhhh, shit.

Behind her, a scream rang out and Alice ducked behind the van, coming into hard communion with the wall and rattling her teeth in the process. The scream cut off as a growl tore across it, echoing off the pillars and ceiling.

Her back against the wall, Alice tried to slide down into a sitting position, but the vehicle was backed in too close. Alice crept from behind the vehicle and seated herself on the concrete first before inching her way into the gap.

Her breathing came harsh and ragged.

Please, no.

Willing herself to breathe though her nose, she forced herself to be quiet, to be *very* quiet.

Farther away and out of sight, the growling had stopped, now replaced by a thick ripping sound, along with a dragging along the floor. Alice raised her hands to the bumper and gripped as tightly as she could. Sweat from earlier that evening now chilled her, a tide of goose bumps creeping over her skin.

Smacking sounds now, along with sporadic growls.

Alice remembered the pattern of Kieran's shirt when he crouched in front of her, and screwed her eyes shut.

I will end you.

Oh, God.

Her hands hooked into claws, she dug her nails into the bumper as though that would preserve her hold on life. One nail bent, and Alice gritted her teeth against the discomfort. Her teeth bared in a wretched grimace, Alice strained to hear beyond the smacking sounds. A visceral splatter echoed along the floor, and Alice flinched. *No footsteps. Why weren't there any other footsteps, what about some fucking footsteps?!*

She rested her forehead against the back of the vehicle, the metal cool against her skin, the smell of oil and old linen coming from beyond the back doors. Alice pushed her head against the metal, forcing herself to focus. Given the time of day as well as the location of the car park, there should be people coming in and out, unless there was a reason for them not to, a big fucking reason!! *But that can't last, if the…* She swallowed hard. Even mentally, she couldn't bring herself to admit to using that word, *even if that THING is here, it will have to leave sooner or later, too many people, soon there will be people to scare it off, PLEASE scare it off.*

And even as the thoughts ran through her mind in an increasingly incoherent jumble, one thought rose to the fore: This wasn't just any animal.

I'm not done with you by a long shot.

The look in his eyes when he said that was one of fury; he could barely unclench his teeth to say it to her.

She began to hyperventilate. This close to the back of the van, her breath drifted back on her face, warm and misty, and she turned to the side—

Animal eyes, glaring at her.

Alice recoiled so hard the back of her skull hit the wall, and only the fact that she was already wedged into a tight space prevented her from building up enough momentum to knock herself unconscious.

The animal stood at one side of the van, looking at her over its lowered snout, the fur of its muzzle and chest wet and viscous. The head turned this way and that, the eyes never blinking. Further back along the way she came, a cry of alarm.

Alice whimpered and the animal slid its bulk up against the wall with a whisper of fur brushing over concrete. Lupine eyes widened and the skin of the muzzle twitched, the nostrils flaring. This close, the smell of blood and viscera was cloying.

The head pushed forward, the metal of the van

door rubbing loudly against it, tearing a sob from Alice in the process. She leaned to the side as far as she dared—somewhere in a crowded corner of her mind she realised what little safety she had would be gone completely if she made a run for it.

The animal pushed forward further until it came to a stop inches away. Eyes still glaring at Alice, it planted its paws, the scrabble of claws coming from further back as it fought for traction. The metal of the van door dimpled with a hollow thump, and the creature trembled, moving no further. A rumbling in its chest rose to a growl and the muzzle wrinkled back from its teeth in a snarl, dripping with drool.

"Oh, no, oh, no, oh, no…"

The growl built in crescendo as the jaws opened, the animal roaring at her. Hot ferric breath washed Alice's face, spraying spittle. Between the back of the van and the wall, the sound, already loud, was amplified to a near-deafening level.

"*Jesus fucking Christ!*" A voice from yards away— and the growl subsequently cut short in a snarl.

Alice bit her lip, her heart hammering in her chest. Multiple footsteps sounded from a number of directions.

Fur over the animal's eyes creased in a scowl before metal creaked and the animal pulled free with a visible effort. It angled its head for one final look at Alice before pivoting and bounding off to a chorus of gasps and murmurs.

Alice remained where she was, whimpering.

Shivering.

Bloody spittle drying on her face.

Around her, voices continued to murmur and converse, with some footsteps weaving a path around vehicles. More footsteps paused before walking alongside the van and coming to a stop at the wall.

"Oh, my God," came a whisper.

Alice turned and looked up. A squat and burly man with backcombed hair peered into the gap, his forearm resting along the edge of the van. "Are you hurt, are you okay?" The accent sounded thick; Italian, maybe.

Swallow. Think. Focus. Her heart pounded, but less so than before. Alice looked him in the eyes and gave a slow nod.

The man gave a thin smile in return. "Okay, that's good," he said, his voice lightening with relief. "Here," he said, holding out his hand, "let me help you."

Alice let him take her hand, his meaty paw pulling firmly but gently. She heaved a sigh of relief as she slid from the back of the vehicle and up to her feet, teetering slightly. The man made no attempt to move toward her, rather, he just pushed back on her hand to help her steady herself. She glanced back at the area behind the van, noting a few droplets of blood, nothing more.

She felt her hand lower as the man stepped in closer and circled into her field of vision. "Can you walk?" he asked.

She nodded and swallowed. "Yeah," she murmured. "I can walk."

The man led her past the van, where a younger man stood watching, his thumbs hooked into the back pockets of his jeans. He started forward, but the older man stayed him with a hint of a smile and a tight shake of the head. Alice made eye contact with him, and soon determined the relationship between the two men. She turned back to the man leading her.

"We've all been keeping watch," he said, before giving her hand a small squeeze. Alice winced a little, not so much because of the force of the grip but the suggestion that it could easily have been a lot stronger. Her saviour turned to the younger man and spoke briefly in what Alice guessed would have been Italian, since the only word she could pick out was 'Julio.'

The younger man headed toward one end of the car park where a small group of people were waiting. Animated conversation ensued with Julio gesturing over his shoulder in Alice's direction. Alice watched them a while before turning away, but the man holding her hand stood fast. When she tried to step past him, he matched her step.

"Can we go now?" she said, her voice steadier than before.

The man pulled a face like he had sucked juice from a lemon. "Not that way, you can't."

Alice huffed, now feeling the hand around hers growing slick with sweat. "Really. Wha…?"

The memory of cowering behind the van. A blood-smeared muzzle.

"I…" Did she? Really, *did* she? She held his gaze and swallowed. "I want to see."

The man grew solemn. His lips parted, and Alice heard a gentle clack as though the man have paused for thought mid-chew on a piece of chewing gum. "I don't think you do," he said, lips still parted (and now Alice caught a whiff of gum chewed mintless long since).

"I need to see what happened." She jerked her chin in the direction behind his shoulder. "That could have been me. Okay?"

The man shrugged and stepped back from Alice, although he still held on to her hand. Alice walked back the way she came, closing the distance on a large group up ahead, glows in the darkness coming from the crowd's smartphones. As she drew nearer, more detail became apparent: a couple of the onlookers wore the centre uniforms, the high-heeled foot of a woman lying on her back, dark spatters on the concrete. One onlooker turned to look over her shoulder at Alice, sad eyes set close together in a young face of dusky skin. The woman backed away, and Alice looked at the ground before her.

Splatters of blood surrounded the woman on the floor, her sightless eyes staring beyond Alice's head. Some drops of blood had streaked up over her cheek. Further down, a frock lay torn open, as did the abdomen beneath it. Inside, a glistening cavity trailed a broken loop of intestine onto the ground.

"Someone," Alice muttered. She looked at the remains on the ground.

And coughed, numb lips pursing at the taste of bile.

This time, the man who ushered her to the scene stepped behind her and, grabbing her shoulder, turned her away from both the crowd and the body. As Alice bent, the man swept her hair back from her neck.

Alice vomited, prompting a couple of gasps from behind her, and only when she had reached the dry heaves did the man's hand on her shoulder give her a gentle pat. Cold sweat broke out on her forehead and she raised a hand to it, palming it away. More than cool, her hand felt greasy with sweat. Sickly.

Goose bumps rose in Alice's skin.

Shivering now.

Bent over this close to the floor, sound amplified and echoed around her. Conversation behind her. Footsteps far off, coming closer. The conversation by walkie-talkie, one side clear, the other heavy with static.

Shivering more now.

Sweat oozed from her temples, threatening to roll down her face. Alice prayed that wouldn't happen.

On the pavement in front of her, pedestrians, tourists and shoppers alike walked by, and Alice watched them with bored indifference. The temptation was to hover outside the store looking in, but she didn't have to. She *shouldn't* have to.

The sun's glare from the window of a passing bus dazzled her for a moment and she squinted before raising a hand to her face. As she lowered her arm, sweat in her armpit proved hot and sticky: a far cry to the chills of yesterday.

"...see, and she wasn't even doing it right, so I thought..."

Alice turned. Fumi and another girl, similar height but a lot thicker, Alice noticed, had exited the store and fallen in line with the crowd.

Alice pushed off from the glass and with a murmur of 'excuse me', groped her way around a lanky t-shirted man in shades and flip-flops before grabbing Fumi by the arm. Fumi whirled, her expression blank. "Would you take your hand off me, please?"

"NO."

Alice dragged Fumi by the arm back to the Debenhams storefront, pivoted her, and slammed her back against the glass, with some bystanders both in and outside the store slowing to look. Alice clapped a hand on Fumi's shoulder, pinning the girl in place.

The friend sidled up to her. "Did you grow up in a cave or something? Don't you—"

"Wait your turn," Alice snapped, glaring over her shoulder at the girl. "Or I swear I'll punch a hole right through the back of your *fucking* head! Open that fat mouth again and see if I don't."

"Who do you—"

"*Don't fucking tempt me, child!*" she hissed.

The girl shut her mouth, her face sullen. Alice turned her attention back to Fumi, who remained still during the episode.

"Would you take your hand off me, please?" she repeated.

"No, I will not 'take my hand off you'," Alice snapped. "You can stand there and sulk and listen to what I have to say and stop acting like a fucking twat. You might have more experience in a fucking shop, but I can guarantee that you don't have more life experience than me. So shut up and listen."

Fumi slanted an eye-roll at nothing in particular, exhaling a sigh. "I'm listening," she said, eyebrows lifting in prompt. For the wide-eyed vacant look and the set of her jaw, the girl looked like she was chewing gum.

Alice shook her hung head, feeling some of the rage dissipate with her outburst. "You don't know me," she said. "But I'm gonna give you some insight. Years ago, I made a stupid mistake: a very stupid one. I falsely accused someone of rape, which was a stupid and despicable thing to do. I'm not proud of it—I mean, who would be?"

"I know." Again, Fumi's eyebrows lifted in

prompt. "Go on."

She knows. Hardly surprising, given the girl's attitude in general, but it was the ease of admittance that halted Alice for a moment. She pressed on. "Okay. So I went to jail for my mistake, and deservedly so. But know this: that is all behind me now. I've done my time for that same mistake and I'm moving on with life, which isn't easy." The memory and *shame* of cowering behind a van had pushed some of her fear to fury. "So let's get this clear. I don't know what your beef is with me, but if you really can't speak up like some kind of adult and tell me what's bugging you, you need to shelve that shit. Because I've just about had it up to here with you," she said, jabbing her fingertips against her temple. "You hear me? Up to *here*." She swallowed hard. "I've tried to make amends… so…"—and she grit her teeth as her voice cracked —"… just cut me some slack. *Please.*" Less a question and more a declaration.

Fumi cocked her head, her expression still neutral. Her hand still on the girl's shoulder, Alice could feel there was good muscle tone: the girl was fit (with the budding curves of adolescence), but no challenge if she wanted to go head to head in a fight. The other one had mass, but that looked to be about it; from the look of her, a flight of five steps would put her down for the count. At least she had taken that stupid sulk off her face.

"Done?" Fumi asked.

"Yes. I'm done."

"Good. Would you take your hand off me, please?"

Alice complied, inwardly swearing at herself as Fumi, a faint smile on her lips, pushed away from the glass. Swallowing pride, for Alice, was prickly at best, and right now, her insides churned with anxiety. And shame; yes, more shame.

"There's nothing you want to say?" To her own ears, her voice sounded fractured and weak.

Fumi shrugged a shoulder. "I don't have anything to say to you," she said, her tone bright. With that, she tapped her friend on the arm and the two walked away, the friend looking over her shoulder at Alice and beaming at her.

"Byeeee!" The mocking lilt was painfully apparent, and a man walking in the other direction followed the source of the comment, his expression quizzical.

Alice herself now backed against the glass and, deep in thought, clapped a hand over her mouth.

That could have gone better.

Now her eyes burned with tears.

Now every working day going forward would be worse; if that was even possible.

Yards away, the slap of flip-flops interrupted her reverie.

What really bugged Alice wasn't so much the fact that the altercation didn't have the desired outcome, but it was the fact that even after causing a scene (shock and awe, in military terms), Fumi was just as indifferent as before. No more, no less. That was just adding insult to injury. Just like the idiot making a whole lot of fucking noise in the flip-flops, not coming or going anywhere. Alice looked in contempt... and swayed, momentarily lightheaded.

Further down the street beyond the entrance to the next store, Kieran strolled through the crowd toward her, clapping, and held his hands clasped as he crossed the last few feet to her. "I don't think she wants to be your friend anymore," he said, his voice a low rumble in his chest. The corner of his mouth lifted in a half-smile. He leaned in toward her. "And I can't say I blame her either."

His look of disdain on her as he walked past, he melted into the crowd.

Prey.

That's what she was: prey.

And he was stalking his prey. What about his job?

Back at Richard's flat, she curled up on the sofa, wiping the crust of dried tears from her cheeks. Losing a pair of shoes was the least of her worries. Away from the nightmare of echoed car parks, away from the bustle of streets where predators would slip in and out of the crowd undetected, this was where thoughts and fears would chatter away at her. Alice shook her head. Prison was similar in that sense: alone time with your thoughts allowed them off their leashes and let them run wild. Leopards took down gazelles, wolves… wolves picked off sheep. In Alice's case, she had proven even more ineffectual than those animals.

Celeste, nursing a concussion after a blow to the head, reaffirmed that nothing had changed and everything was good between her and Alice. No, she hadn't seen who or what hit her, but at least the injury wasn't life-threatening. *And why should it be?* Alice thought, with a shudder. Kieran wasn't after Celeste. In an effort to make the best of a bad deal, Celeste had invited a couple of girlfriends over to her flat to watch Dinner Date. Alice wasn't invited.

Alice wasn't surprised either.

Naomi had questioned Alice's choices and judgement before, so what was it that she was doing wrong? Not thinking rationally. So where to start?

Alice balled her fist and thumped it slowly against the arm of the sofa, lips pursed in thought. The problem was harassment from a… from someone. The *solution* was easy enough: get him to stop. The all-important question was *how?* Asking him outright was out of the question: if the jaws snapping at her in the car park didn't confirm that, nothing else would. Could she kill him?

Regardless of what she had seen of Kieran (*Jesus fucking Christ*, she thought, *I saw more than I wanted to*), she didn't know if she could kill him, assuming she actually had any opportunity to. If anything, she had brought this situation on herself, whether she wanted to admit it or not. No. She couldn't kill him. But then how to stop him? If she couldn't stop him, would someone else? Why would someone believe her over Kieran?

Oh.

She leaned back in her chair, hand sliding back and forth across her neck.

Ohhh…

Alice pushed from the sofa and walked to the kitchen, her footsteps heavy. Standing on tiptoe, even though the cupboards were well within reach, she opened one door and pulled out an orange from a bag of fruit in the farthest recess. Richard was too slovenly to unpack his groceries completely.

So this is what you're doing now?

Fingers rolling the orange back and forth. Pitted and waxy to the touch.

Remember Naomi? What do you think she'd say?

Alice clasped a hand to her forehead, fingers massaging her temple.

The girl doesn't know shit.

…but I do.

Gritting her teeth, she slid her hand from her forehead over her eyes and squeezed. "Shit…"

Slipping off her cardigan, Alice improvised a makeshift sling with the orange in the sleeve and let it dangle from one hand. She moved to the kitchen door where she braced one hand against the frame, the knuckles of her hands standing out in stark relief. Her heart pounded in her chest, her pulse racing.

Alice exhaled a shaky breath. Her grip trembling.

On three.

She screwed her eyes shut.

One. Two…

She swung the sling upward, the blow catching her hard on the temple—so hard that she momentarily lost her grip on the doorframe. Again she swung at herself, this time at the base of her jaw. Tears sprang to her eyes, and her nails dug into the wood of the doorframe. A final blow across the top of her thigh.

Her work done, Alice padded back to the lounge and eased herself onto the sofa. There she slid the orange out of the sleeve and began to peel, flecks of the orange's skin sticking to her fingers. Both peeling and eating were repetitive and slow; the body on automatic pilot while the mind ran riot through a kaleidoscope of a waking nightmare. A change… a metamorphosis. Bloodied jaws, snapping at her. The promise of threat waiting downwind.

Orange eaten, Alice tucked herself into a corner of the sofa, dropping the pile of peel on the floor. Touching her fingertips to her jaw proved uncomfortable.

Breath shuddered out of her as she stretched out on the sofa and laid her head on the sofa arm.

Trying to ignore the rigidity beneath the fabric.

Only a temporary measure.

PART 3

"Alice?" The voice drifted down through her unconsciousness like the surface call to a diver.

A hand on her shoulder now.

Alice opened her eyes, the lids sore and rough from shallow sleep and spent tears.

Richard looked down at her, the boyish face now set in a mask of concern.

"Alice," he said, "what the f..." He frowned. "What the hell happened to you?"

Alice braced a hand against the arm of the sofa and Richard gently slid a hand under her bicep, helping her up. His grip felt loose but warm.

She sat upright and looked down at the floor, as Richard moved to the other side of the sofa and sat down beside her. She looked over her shoulder at him, and gave him a sad smile, aggravating a tight soreness at the base of her jaw.

"Alice? Who hit you?"

Eyes downcast.

"Kieran?" he asked.

She met his gaze as her breath hitched, and she shrugged.

"Motherfucker."

Richard leaned forward, his elbows on his knees and his hands dangling. Wary curiosity on his face: his gaze intense, and his eyebrows lifting in encouragement.

"I think he followed me," Alice said. "I was out with Celeste, you know, my friend from the bank? So we went to the bank—sorry, I mean we went up to…" She bit her lip. "I feel so stupid," she said. Now her voice cracked. She hung her head, blonde hair hanging in a veil around her face. Through the haze of strands she saw Richard turn toward her, dipping his head to make eye contact with her.

Tears came slowly at first with the effort of pushing the body through an unnatural state. Caricaturing the mouth into a frown of tearful grief almost felt genuine. More tears came now, more freely. "So we went for some lunch, just because we were catching up and talking about Becca's wedding, you know? He…he must have been watching me and following me, because by the time I was there in the car park, he'd already found me."

Cushions of the sofa dipped as Richard shifted closer toward her. The skin of his bare arm was cool, the size of his arm comforting as he draped it over her shoulders.

"I told him that he was scaring me, but he didn't

want to know… you know?" She lifted her head and sighed. Sniffled. "He said…"

I'm not done with you by a long shot.

She gave a weary chuckle. "He grabbed my face in his hand," she said, miming the action, "and said I have much to answer for."

Richard gave a slow headshake. "Sick. That's just sick."

Alice shrugged one shoulder as she gave a sniffle. A cough, sputtering a little. "Maybe it's me. Maybe in the middle of it all, he's got a point."

"No," Richard said firmly. "Even if it was wrong, that's in the past now. It doesn't give him the right to drag that shit up now, let alone put his hands on you for it. He's less than a man, acting like that."

Tentatively, Richard placed a finger under her chin and turned her face toward his, peering along the length of her jaw. "I'm guessing it feels worse than it looks. The bruising doesn't look so bad though. I'm guessing it'll go down in a couple of days."

"Really?"

"Yeah, looks like you're gonna be okay."

"A couple of days." She sat up, looked at the ceiling and scoffed. "I feel like shit right now. I know I look like shit."

"No, you don't. You're just a little shaken, and that's understandable. That's what he's put you through. But you don't need to worry about him anymore," he said softly.

"Honestly. I feel like shit, I look like shit—"

"No," he said, planting his hands on her shoulders. "Alice, you're okay. On the inside as well as the outside. I know you're not perfect: dumping rind on my carpet, for one," he said, gesturing at the orange peel on the floor, prompting a teary laugh from Alice, "but you tick a lot of boxes. You'll be fine."

Alice sniffled and wrung her hands in her lap. "You know…" She rested a hand on his knee and licked her lips. "I didn't think I would see any way out of this, but after talking to you, I feel safe."

"You *are* safe," he said. His eyes widened a little as his mouth drew into a tight line. *"Trust me."*

Alice raised a hand to Richard's face and cupped his cheek in her palm, his gaze flickering. "You're a good friend," she said. "Thank you." And with another sniffle, she leaned in and threw her arms around his neck, hugging him. His hands came to rest on her hips. This close to the hollow of his neck, the smell of Lynx deodorant was evident on his skin; at least pleasant, if not seductive. Pressed cheek to cheek, she drew her lips along the line of his jaw and up to his lips and kissed him—a quick peck.

Her arms still hung around his neck.

But Richard just sat there.

Alice leaned in, but Richard's grip on her hips tightened, staying her in place.

He gave a slow shake of his head.

Alice's breath caught and she sniffled, her lips curving in a bitter smile.

They soon parted company with Richard reassuring her that she could go to bed and that he would straighten the place up. While Alice had suspected that Richard's interest in her might be more than platonic, the fact that he wasn't thinking with his dick brought genuine tears to her eyes. There were still people out there who cared—good people. Those were the kind of people you needed to keep close and look after.

Richard knocked on the glass of the front door, prompting the man at the desk inside the lounge to look up. To Richard, the guy looked like the type that would probably knock oh-so-gently at a door with the back of his knuckle. Probably thought the stubbly beard made him look rugged and masculine. Richard thought he looked like a wuss. At least he'd caught the man before closing time—but only just. It looked like everyone else had left.

The man got to his feet and made his way through an arrangement of square and firm leather armchairs, before pulling the door open a fraction.

"Can I help you?" he asked.

"Yeah, I think you can," Richard said, smiling. "I've got a friend who's getting married soon, and she's a bit of a wine enthusiast. So I was hoping that you would..." He shrugged. "You know, show me around a little?"

The man looked unimpressed.

"To be honest," Richard said quickly. "She knows a lot more about wine than I would ever do. She's something of a wine connoisseur. Me, I'm lucky if I can spell the bloody thing, you know?"

The man's chest lifted as he inhaled, and the corner of his mouth lifted into a half smile. Richard dug his hands into his pockets, clasping them tight against his thighs.

"So, yeah," he continued. "She's having a wedding soon. This weekend, in fact, and each member of the bridal party has to weigh in with a surprise. I figured it would be good for me if I did something other than play some music for her: I play a little saxophone," he said as an aside, spreading his hands in supplication as though this would authenticate the lie. "She's kind of refined and likes to experience the finer things in life. So after browsing some stuff on Google, here I am. Spare me a few minutes? I'm prepared to pay for your time."

The man held up a hand as though halting traffic. "Honestly, that won't be necessary. I can make time for a wine enthusiast, Mr...?"

"Richard Greenway," he said, extending his hand.

"Kieran."

The two shook hands before Kieran stood back, pulling the door wide open. Richard stepped in.

"This place looks impressive. The kind of thing that you'd only see on TV, or on cable or something."

Kieran smiled. "There's a whole other world out there. This," he said, flitting a finger in the direction of the ceiling, "is just a small part of the premises. We do have a modest cellar here as well. We work with a basement conversion company who are…"—he smiled through a mock grimace—"pricey… but they do good work. If you want, I can show you now, and if you like what you see? We might arrange a private showing for the bride and/or the bridal party. How does that sound?"

Richard grinned. "Sounds like a plan."

"I'd say so. Follow me."

Kieran led Richard through the back of the lounge area and to a spiral staircase down into a basement. "This is pretty good," Kieran said, flicking on the nearby wall switch.

Dim fluorescent tubing in the arched ceiling revealed one side of the broad passageway racked with barrels of wine, the far end of the passage set with a small wine rack.

"Wow," Richard breathed, stepping up behind Kieran.

"I know. The best part is that this is just a sample of the wines we offer as well as an example of a bespoke wine cellar."

"I do have a confession to make," Richard said.

Kieran stopped short, pivoted. His mouth a half-smile, he cocked his head in curiosity. "A confession."

"Yeah."

He shrugged his shoulders and puckered his lips in thought. "As they say, I'm all ears."

Richard cupped one hand in the other, the thumb digging into the palm. "It's about Alice."

Any trace of humour on Kieran's face melted like butter on a hotplate. He straightened and inhaled deep through his nose. His gaze on the ceiling, his lips parted as though he were working through a length of mental arithmetic, until he spoke at last. "Do you even have an interest in wine?"

"What?" To Richard, the question was spoken clearly, but it simply wasn't expected.

"I said, 'do you even have an interest in wine?'"

"No," Richard said. "I mean, yeah, sure, I like wine,"—and here, Kieran's brows lowered—"but I just wanted to talk to you about Alice."

Kieran slid his hands into his pockets and fixed Richard with a look. "Why?"

"Because she looks like she's taken a beating, is all."

Eyebrows lifting, Kieran's jaw worked as though chewing over a range of responses. "So you think I had something to do with it?"

"No, I don't," Richard said, his voice weary, "and that's just the point." He let the comment sink in, watching as Kieran sized him up. "Look. I know what Alice has put you through and it must have been a living hell. Now she's sporting a bruise or two and saying you had a hand in it. I'd have to be a right muppet to take it on face value."

Kieran gave a slow nod. "Fair point well made."

"So I don't need to ask the obvious question here."

Kieran edged closer. "And what question would that be, pray tell?"

Richard licked his lips.

"What question would that be?"

Richard's heart thudded in his chest. Away from the shop floor upstairs, the cool cellar felt cool and claustrophobic like a tomb. "Did you have a hand in it?"

A half-smile, the eyes devoid of humour. "No. I did not," he said. "Do you have any other questions for me?"

"No, no, no," Richard said, after a sigh. "Maybe Alice hasn't had an easy ride since she's been released from prison, but you didn't have an easy ride either. Any idea why she would be pointing the finger at you?"

"Don't know, don't care."

"Come on," Richard scoffed, "you *must* care. Even if you don't want to admit it, you've gotta be curious about it."

"I'm curious," Kieran said, holding up a forefinger, "as to why *you* care. If she's as despicable as you make out, why don't you cut your losses?"

Richard looked him in the eye, his stare wavering

like a candle flame in a breeze before dropping his gaze. "I made an effort when a lot of people wanted nothing to do with her." The stare gave way to resignation. "I guess I didn't want to look so stupid at the end of it all."

Kieran's mouth drew into a thin line and he gave a tight shake of the head. "Cupid's arrow. I should've guessed. If I were you, I'd cut my losses, cut her loose completely and move on. If you want to see if the grass is greener on the other side, just read my backstory. I'm sure there'll be a tabloid or two that will present you with the whole sordid affair. There might even be a picture or two." He rested a hand on Richard's arm, ushering him back to the stairway, but Richard stood his ground.

Kieran turned his gaze to the other man, one eye half closing.

"Look. I just want to know why Alice isn't leaving you alone."

"Maybe you should be asking her. *Now* would be good."

As Richard turned and headed for the stairs, Kieran came up behind him, reaching for his arm. Richard, caught unawares, spun, knocking Kieran off balance and spilling him to the floor. Kieran pushed to his hands and knees, his back heaving. Richard stepped off the last riser and drew alongside Kieran as he began to crawl to the far wall.

Halting midway, Kieran coughed; a thick

rumbling cough from deep in his chest that was almost phlegmatic. Richard watched as the other man's back bowed, the shirt pulled taut over the shoulders. *Is he sick?*

"Shit," Richard muttered, stooping by Kieran's shoulders. "Sorry, man. Are you okay?"

And Kieran's head snapped up.

Confusion was Richard's first response; then his eyes widened in horror.

Kieran's nose darkened, the upper lip cleaving down the middle. His forehead rose and fell like something pulsed within. Snaps and pops like the continued cracking of knuckles came from all over: his face, his body, his arms and legs. Richard sat down hard, jarring his spine in the process, transfixed open-mouthed by the horror in front of him.

The twitching and shifting figure in front of Richard groaned, and it sounded more like a *growl*, echoing off the stone walls. The head lifted, and Richard could see the shirt tightening over the arms and shoulders until it started to tear. The muzzle split into a pair of fanged jaws and the animal growled, the voice thick and guttural. Dim light directly overhead only revealed the ends of the figure's fur pushing through the tattered shirt; the rest of the shape remained in shadow.

The cracks and snaps were fewer now. Soon silence returned.

Snarling cut through the air, wicked fangs

revealing themselves in shadow.

The animal pounced, the head hitting Richard in the gut like a wrecking ball. Richard brought his hands up and slapped them against the creature's head and shoved, but the muzzle worried back and forth, buffeting his hands away. Teeth tore through Richard's shirt and into his stomach and he gasped, the pinch on his abdomen akin to a stitch from running, magnified a hundred fold. The animal bit deeper and, rearing up on its hind legs, swung Richard into the wall before letting him drop to the floor, the impact smacking the back of his skull against the concrete. Jaws clamped on his stomach again and yanked until the skin tented and tore, pulling loose and releasing a gout of blood.

Amid Richard's screams, the animal tore through muscle and into thick steaming viscera.

Soon the screams stopped.

Along with the dragging of mutilated flesh, the growling continued.

Silence.

Blessed peace.

The smell of red wine.

More so, the smell of viscera and blood, thick and ferric. Hanging in the air above him like an invisible cloud formation.

Kieran lay on his back with his forearm over his eyes, his hunger sated somewhat. The urge to break the overhead light and plunge the cellar into darkness was tempting, but then that would be more mess to clean up. Currently there was enough mess to clean up.

He pushed up and sat cross-legged, exhaling a sigh as he looked about himself. Blood smeared his skin from head to toe (and he could feel it gluing his hair together in places), some patches on the floor thicker than others, soaking into shredded clothing that lay about. Arcs and spatters of blood marked the lower reaches of the cellar walls. Piles of viscera, intestine or otherwise, lay here and there, along with raggedly severed limbs. He glanced over his shoulder. One forearm lay nearby, the hand at the farther end of the severed limb, palm up and the fingers curled loosely as if accepting spare change.

Kieran growled and shifted his position, groping behind him. Something larger and bulkier. Securing a handhold, he brought the object into his lap, his fingers curled into Richard's mouth, his thumb under Richard's jaw, Richard's glassy eyes fixed on a point over Kieran's shoulder. One upper arm jutted from his torso, the rest of the body bitten through and torn away below the ribcage.

Kieran hefted the mass in his hand, and gave the head a withering look.

Alice.

Her scent was all over this kid.

Growling, Kieran swung the torso in a backhand, hitting the wall in a fleshy smack. Droplets of blood sprayed. Again he swung it, and again, until he heard something splinter inside the torso.

Fucking Alice.

Somewhat spent, he hefted the torso back into his lap and turned it over. Richard's eyes looked past him, frozen in fright.

Hmmmm.

Gripping it by the back of its neck, Kieran hefted Richard's torso up to face him. For all the savagery of the last hour, the face was surprisingly unmarked.

Little over a year ago, he wouldn't have thought anything like this evening was possible, until an attempted mauling one night had proven him wrong. Clawed and bitten, adrenaline had boosted him into a dumpster and saved him from death by dismemberment. Feelings of restlessness sat with him for the next two weeks until his body did something wholly unexpected and *changed*. As painful as it was unpredicted, but the high that came from taking down his first victim felt like an orgasm. And through remorse, both sides of him soon developed a begrudging mutual awareness, since survival depended on it. Knowing that there would be consequences had prompted Kieran to take action: buying shipyard chain, padlocks and a muzzle. They wouldn't stop the change, but at least they would restrain him, while he could develop a degree of control.

And he had.

But now?

Restraint was unnecessary. No wolf should need to apologise for picking off sheep.

Lifting Richard's torso, Kieran sank his teeth into the neck, chewing slowly.

Fuck consequences.

Naomi exited the car and swung the driver's side door shut, clicking the key fob. Not only did she make it back to the house in good time (which meant time to relax) but it also meant more time to ensure that place was as it should be for when Kazu came over. She made her way up the street, thinking ahead: the wine in the fridge, the black leather mules to slip on for when he…

Oh, hello.

The man leaning outside her front gate had an air of nonchalance about him, but something Naomi couldn't quite put her finger on was disquieting. Unconsciously, she slowed her approach. As she drew nearer, she could make out more of the stranger's appearance: medium height, slim. Holding what looked like a Hotel Chocolat bag in his lap. Well-dressed, with a paisley print shirt open at the collar, and slacks.

Still, a good offence was a good defence.

"Can I help you?" Naomi asked as she closed the distance between them, her tone casual.

The stranger turned. "You're Naomi, right?" he asked, holding his hand out.

"I am," she said, shaking the offered hand. "And you are?"

"Kieran."

OH.

"Is Alice here?" he said, waving a finger at the house. "Only I've been waiting here for a while and I rang the doorbell, but no answer. Figured I'd take a chance on waiting and see if she happened by. Haven't seen her at work lately."

"Sorry, there's no Alice living here," Naomi replied, her tone curt. She made her way around him to open the gate, but his hand came down on it, holding it closed.

"But she used to live here, right? At least for a while?"

Those who knew Naomi could count calm under fire as one of her strengths, along with multitasking on a La Marzocco espresso machine. What she couldn't and wouldn't do was lie.

"She used to, yeah."

Kieran's mouth curved in a half smile. "Did she tell you about me?"

Naomi met his gaze. "Yes, she did."

He grimaced as though tasting pure lemon juice. "Yeah, well, don't believe everything you're told."

Naomi looked down at his hand. "Would you mind letting go of the gate, please?"

"So here's a question," Kieran continued. "If she's not here living here now, where is she?"

She looked up at him. "Couldn't tell you," she

said.

"Couldn't? Or wouldn't?"

"You pick. She's cut me off."

Something… *rusty* caught in the breeze, the scent both subtle and unexpected. If Kieran smelled it, he gave no outward sign of it.

Kieran glanced away for a moment, his lips pursed in thought. When he turned back, the smile was gone. "Let me set the record straight here," he said. "I don't know what Alice has told you, but she has a problem with me," he said, wagging a finger under his chin.

"I wouldn't know anything about that," she said, dismissing it with a facial shrug.

"I wouldn't expect you to. So when you say that Alice isn't here anymore, I believe you. When you say that you don't know where she is, I believe you."

"Right. I don't know."

Kieran held up a hand. "Let me cut to the chase," he said, leaning in close. "Alice can run and hide all she wants, but her luck is gonna run out soon. When I see her, I'll take a lot more than an apology." He handed Naomi the bag before turning and strolling away.

Prick. Naomi turned and let herself into her flat, heading to the lounge and then dropping onto the sofa. *Why he'd come calling at this time of night is beyond me*, she thought, pulling the bag handles apart. While Alice may have brought—

Dropping the bag, Naomi clapped both hands

over her mouth, screaming against her palms. "*Oh, my God!*"

Richard's eyeless face lay on the bottom of the bag, the skin ragged at the edges of the contoured mask. One side of the mask was torn through the cheek, leaving a flap of skin curled underneath one of the eyeholes. It looked surreal, like a prop from a selection of Halloween costumes: blatant and ugly. Splotches of faded blood dotted the bottom of the bag.

"Oh... oh..." Words wouldn't come, and the surreal nature of this... *thing* in the bag...

Naomi looked away. This time of the evening, the dark blue of night, a shade lighter over the horizon, had yet to deepen. The occasional car would cruise by one of the adjacent streets, or some conversation subdued by four walls would drift from the neighbouring houses.

Tears pricked at Naomi's eyes and she fidgeted on the sofa.

Richard was dead.

Murdered.

Mutilated.

With the silence and loss came another sensation.

Naomi sat up, the tears drying on her face. Apart from the ticking of the clock on the wall, the flat was silent. From the kitchen, a faint dripping of the tap over the sink. The faint hum of electricity.

Fingers crawling to her waist, Naomi pulled her smartphone from her pocket and dialled, her hearing focused elsewhere all the while. Moments later, a woman's voice, cordial and automated, told her the number was unavailable. Naomi tried the number again. And again, the same automated voice told her the number was unavailable. Sending a text message gave no indication of success. Had Alice blocked her? Could Naomi blame her if she had?

Naomi laid the phone in her lap, sitting alone in the gloom and listening to the silence inside the flat, and the silence outside.

All thoughts of Kazu forgotten.

Thoughts of Alice foremost in her mind.

To a round of applause, Rebecca and Beresford sealed their marriage with their first kiss as husband and wife. The procession down the aisle of the church hall in Chiswick was a relief for both of them, which they would happily tell the guests about when they made it outside into the freshness of a Saturday afternoon. Dull grey skies overhead held out against rain and by the time the wedding party had made it to the hired bus and a fleet of taxis, late afternoon had brought sun to the grounds of the Bingham hotel.

Alice made her way through the crowd and chatter, a half-full champagne flute in hand. Since bruising herself a couple of days earlier, the marks had faded enough for make-up to mask them to all but the most keen observer. Booking into the Bingham had been costly but this way, she'd be closer to family—if only for a while. With the lift in appearance (and an even nicer pair of shoes than the ones lost) came a lift in attitude, and so Alice found herself breezing through the crowd, clinking her glass against that of the nearest guest. Even when finally meeting her mother, standing tall with the usual bob now reaching her shoulders, Alice received a strained smile. That there was any smile at all suggested that fences might mend in time.

An older woman in a skirt suit and lace-veiled hat stood with her back to Alice and following a tap on the arm, the woman stepped aside with a murmured, 'of course.' Alice came round to Rebecca's side. "Still got a long a day ahead," she said, raising her glass and clicking it against Rebecca's own.

"Sure do. But at least the worst of it's behind me. Good thing the weather's holding though. If anything, it's actually improved. I thought it was going to rain earlier for sure."

"Yeah, you and me both."

Reaching low, Alice took Rebecca's hand in her own, the fingers lacing together.

"Sis?"

"Hmmm?"

Alice opened her mouth to speak but faltered. So many things to say, all of them jostling for first place.

Rebecca tightened her grip on her sister's hand. "Hey," she whispered.

"I wish I had what you do. Have," she said with a sniffle. "I love you."

Rebecca's eyes misted. "Love you, too." She shook Alice's hand. "You just keep moving forward, okay?"

Alice gave a wink, a tentative smile in place.

"How does it feel?"

"Feels pretty good."

"Mmmm, say that again," said a voice behind Rebecca. Strong dark hands slid up from behind her, over her hips and settled over her belly. Beresford rested his chin on her shoulder and kissed her on the cheek, pulling his bride back into him as she laughed. With his short dreads and shaven short back and sides, he looked sharper than usual.

"I have to admit," he said, "that she feels pretty good. I feel pretty blessed, truth be told."

"Baby, we're both blessed," Rebecca said, leaning back into him and kissing him on the cheek.

Hubbub dwindled away as a fingernail flicked against a half-full champagne flute. The man in question bore similarity to Beresford apart from a leaner build and a cleanly shaven head. "Ladies and gentlemen," he began. "Ladies and gentlemen. Excuse me while I interrupt the canapé part of the afternoon. If we can get the rest of the family—and my lecherous brother—down to the garden for some pictures with Rebecca's family as well, that would be good."

The crowd parted and shifted in places as the immediate family of both Rebecca and Beresford made their way down the stone steps to the lush grass of the garden area. Both on the grass and from the balcony, photographers and guests held up their cameras and smartphones, taking a number of shots. Between pictures, Alice sucked in her cheeks, puckering repeatedly as she wore a bug-eyed expression: acts of the little sister who would be the eternal child to her older sibling. Rebecca gave Alice's hand a double squeeze, staying her for the moment.

Afternoon eventually gave way to the evening, as the wine and champagne flowed, as waist-coated staff ferried canapé trays of mini sausages, goat's cheese and more through the crowd. By now, more guests had arrived for the reception and inside the main room, the accordion door partition had been pulled back to create a small banqueting room, complete with round tables under heavy white table cloth, place card holders (with the names randomly sorted so that guests would get to know each other) and gleaming silverware. As earlier in the day, Beresford's brother Romeo stood with a half-full glass in hand and tapped a teaspoon against the side of it.

"Ladies and gentlemen. Ladies and gentlemen," he said, allowing the chatter to subside. "First of all, thank you for coming, and for spending time on this special day, the wedding of Beresford and Rebecca. I always thought that I would be the one to get married first, and Lord knows it wasn't for lack of trying." Laughter rose from the crowd. "But in more ways than one, Big Brother took his time. When I was failing at maths in school, he took his time to show me how it was done right. When I didn't get it the first time around, the second or third time around, again—he took his time to show me how it was done right. When I was out in the real world, looking for my first job, I came back with a lot of rejections. You know the old catch twenty-two. Employers wouldn't hire you unless you had experience, and you wouldn't get experience unless someone would hire you. But still, Beresford would have none of it. He'd sit me down and listen and listen and listen, and only when I finished? Then he'd tell me how it was done right. Patience and dedication was key."

The crowd solemn, some nodding, sat enraptured.

"So now," Romeo continued, "it's something a little different. This is where Beresford is going into new days with his lovely wife. But what I can say is that for a lifetime of you standing by me, I have no doubt that your marriage will follow as so many things in your life have. It'll be done right." He held up his glass. "To the bride and groom."

"To the bride and groom," the guests chorused, with some of them standing to clink their glasses against those of others.

Alice's mother stood up. "I guess," she said, "that in the interest of equality and all that, I should say something about the bride. After all, I carried her for nine months. Although given how much of a terror she was," she said, her expression deadpan, "it sometimes felt like ten." Laughter rose in the crowd and Rebecca clapped her hand to her mouth in joyous alarm as Beresford slid an arm around her shoulders.

"But I do want to thank everyone for coming, to spend this time with the couple on their special day. I think you'll agree that Rebecca looks beautiful. Beresford, I can see from the look on your face that you agree too. Just remember, she's still my daughter." Again, laughter rose from the crowd, this time with scattered applause. "But all joking aside, this good man makes my daughter happy and she obviously makes him happy. So I wish you both continued happiness in a long and joyful marriage. To the bride and groom," she said, raising her glass. The guests echoed the sentiment, again clinking glasses with their neighbours.

With that, the guests returned to conversations at their tables, some of them stepping out onto the patio for a smoke in the night air. Alice turned her attention back to her starter of mushroom tartlet, poking at it with her fork. It looked like an apricot Danish, except the filling was grey. Alice pulled a wan face. The filling should either be sweet or meat, and this was neither. Still, as a guest—and one who wasn't footing the bill—the least she could do was eat it. She sliced the end off the tartlet and forked it into her mouth. Rich flavour and oily texture in return.

"Good?"

She looked up at the man seated next to her, thinning blond hair combed into a left-hand parting. "It's not bad."

"No, it isn't. Although, you're looking at a little surprised that it is." He gave a sly smile, his gaze half-lidded. "Are you a meat lover?"

Alice let his words sink in. *Meat lover.* "You could say that, yeah."

"You and me both. There are plenty of vegetarians and vegans out there, so far be it from me to deprive of them of the joy of living meat-free. I'm more than happy to pick up the slack for them," he said, punctuating the air with his knife before laying his cutlery against his plate. He offered his hand. "Shane."

"Alice," she said, returning the greeting.

Shane glanced at his plate and picked up his knife and fork again before continuing. "So I know what brings you here, but who exactly is it? Someone on the bride's side or—"

Glass shattered in a resounding crash as the patio doors blew inward, a body smacking into the nearest table and sending it flying into its neighbours. Food and drink flew in the process, as plates, cutlery and glasses crashed to the floor. Guests rose to their feet, shouting, screaming and backing away while behind them, other guests including Alice and Shane craned their necks toward the commotion. Both exchanged a glance before making their way to the gathering near the patio. Alice peered over the shoulder of one man, her eyes widening.

Next to an overturned table, one of the male guests lay on his back with his eyes wide and vacant, his head lolling at an unnatural angle. Skin from his neck lay wide open in a tattered flag, the inside a mess of dark bloody viscera. Blood leaking from the man's throat stained the white of his shirtfront a bib that glistened under the lights. Another man crouched by the dead man's head, his hand cupping his face as he wept. Behind him, Rebecca and Beresford. Alice met her sister's gaze and saw confusion. Horror.

A growl—thick and loud—cut through the night air beyond the patio steps.

Murmurs and gasps rose from the throng. Alice's vision swam, her heart thudding in her chest.

Conversation came in harsh whispers. "Holy shit."

"What the *fuck* is it?"

"Don't move. If you stay still, it might go away."

"Fuck off. If you stay, you end up like him."

Overhead, the lights went out, plunging the room into darkness and a scream came from the far side of the room. A sniffle too, from the weeping man.

"Shut up!" a voice hissed.

"Both of you shut up before I do it for you." Another voice, deeper than the last.

Whispers now from around the room: "It turned off the lights."

Near Alice, a woman swore under her breath.

"No! Maybe if we keep calm, it will get bored and go away. We don't want to excite it any more."

An upturned table rolled slowly on its circumference as Rebecca, crouched in her wedding dress, drew the improvised shield in front of her. When she waved her hand at the man nearest to her, he followed suit and rolled another table toward hers, forming a makeshift barrier.

"Everyone listen," Rebecca said, her voice low. "A-a-as slowly as you can, lay flat on the floor. No matter what you do, no sudden moves—none at all. Okay? Do it now."

Rustling and shuffling broke the silence as shoes scraped along the floor, with the occasional crunch of glass or squelch of food underfoot.

Another growl, closer now.

The head crested the top of the stone stairs at the far end of the patio. The body soon followed. From what Rebecca could see, peering over the edge of the table, it looked like a dog or a wolf but it was too big to be either. It padded closer, ears twitching, fur bristling. The eyeshine grew clearer with each step, flickering as the animal blinked. Its muzzle appeared dark and wet against the night.

It loped inside the room, glass and splinters of wood skating aside with its passage.

Rebecca gripped onto the stem of the table in front of her, keeping her gaze low on the animal's paws.

The muzzle lifted high and swung through a slow arc in the air.

Turning, the animal bounded out onto the patio and disappeared down the steps and into the darkness.

Silence fell over the room.

With the silence came the clarity of other senses: the silhouettes of upturned tables and the guests that lay among them. The smell of food and wine.

And that of blood.

The man holding the table next to Rebecca's looked back over his shoulder at the room. "Everyone okay back there?"

Gradually, the group murmured their assent as they rose to their feet. As the lights were switched on, the guests made their way through the crowd, shaken and subdued. When they found their relatives and loved ones, they clasped them and asked for reassurances that they were okay. Rebecca took Beresford's hand in her own and held it to her cheek. Tears welled in her eyes and he pulled her close to steady her trembling as well as his own.

He stroked a hand through her hair. "You scared me," he whispered.

She nodded against his chest. "I'm sorry," she sobbed. "I was scared. God, I was so scared."

"Me, too."

He held her as she cried against his chest, soaking his shirt with her tears and a trickle of mucus from her nose. Done at last, she pushed away from him and looked to the scene on the floor. The man who sobbed previously now sat by the head of the dead man, a similarly blank look on his own face; motionless apart from the slow passage of tears and gentle rise and fall of his back. Rebecca started forward, and Beresford's hand clamped on her own. She spun back to question him, only to be met with a tired expression.

"Not now," he whispered. "Right now, I think we should back off."

As stubborn as Rebecca could be, the firm grasp which still held her hand in a vise grip warned that this was not open for debate. The same hand drew her back into the arms of her husband and she shuddered a sigh of relief against the damp of Beresford's shirtfront. His cologne, now thick with the odour of sweat, smelled good: so strong and good.

"Thank you," she breathed.

He kissed the top of her head, his lips warm through her hair.

She eased back from his chest and surveyed the room. Some guests were sitting on chairs next to upturned tables while some stood huddled in groups. A couple stood aside, and Rebecca's mother made her way through the mess, her face lined with worry. Rebecca patted the flat of her hand against Beresford's chest and he released her, where she then hugged her mother. Rebecca's mother pulled away first, looking over one shoulder.

Then the other.

And as realisation dawned on Rebecca, she picked her way through the crowd, scrutinising every face, her anxiety growing.

It didn't help.

The smart thing may have been to hide, what with safety in numbers and such. But, no.

It didn't help.

Alice had fled as soon as the lights went out. Past the kitchen, down the hallway and out into the night, where she discovered the first flaw in the plan: there was no quick getaway. As seemed to be the way for many functions and weddings she had been to in the past, public transportation was minimal, which meant hiring a cab unless you were on good terms with a driver—assuming you yourself didn't drive. The only consolation was that Richmond station was a fifteen-minute walk away. Less time when running full-tilt through darkened streets in a state of panic. While there were some cabs outside the station, those were pre-booked, and Alice didn't dare waste time arguing and causing a scene, which would only draw more attention to her. Now she cowered at the farthest end of the platform from the station entrance, her jacket drawn tight around her and her leather pumps dangling from the fingers of one hand. Not since her last drunken episode on a night out with the girls had she walked the streets barefoot, much less run.

This was all her fault, in the worst possible way. She had cried wolf. Now one had come after her.

It would *keep* coming after her.

Alice looked up at the dot matrix board. Seven minutes for a train into London. Seven minutes, seven, seven minutes, seven minutes…

She looked along the length of the platform. At the far end to her left, the shadowy recesses of the staircase down to the ticket hall. To her right and beyond the edge of the curved mirror, the final slope of the platform into rock, grass and nature.

Seven fucking minutes.

She looked back toward the board.

Six minutes now.

Below her in the track bed, the tracks whispered in metallic tones. Alice looked to her right. In the distance, the front of a train appeared, light glowing from the headlamps and the cabin. Excitement pumped Alice's heart faster as she sat forward on her bench. The train's image grew larger and resolved itself into focus with the blare of a horn. The train hurtled along the platform in a flurry of fluorescent backlit windows and strong wind, the gust of which ruffled Alice's hair. As quick as the train had whipped into the station, it had sped on into the darkness, dwindling away to nothing along the other end of the platform.

Shit.

SHIT.

Alice looked to the board.

Five minutes.

She clasped her knees together, trembling as she rocked back and forth on the bench. On the platform across from her, a crop-haired woman with lace-free Doc Martens sat puffing a cigarette. Further down the same platform was a man wearing a sheepskin jacket and white Nikes.

One young couple further down her platform were wrapped in each other's arms and nuzzling one another. Alice rocked back and forth harder. Ordinarily she wouldn't want people to stand so close to her, especially lone men but now when she needed them, they were all standing as far away as possible. Alice bit her lip. At least at this end, she was out of sight—*hopefully* out of sight. *Hopefully? Oh, God.*

Again, the metallic whispers from the track bed.

Alice looked to her right, again seeing a train pull into view. Much slower than its predecessor as another train slowed up to the opposite platform from the other direction.

Alice looked back to the board.

Two minutes.

Enough time for the train to pull into the station, open the doors for boarding and alighting (*fucking stupid word*, she thought) before shutting up shop and speeding away.

The train pulled into the platform, slowing to a halt. Alice could see life in the carriage: a man reading his book, head bowed. Another man, tall and lean in Lycra shorts, standing in the doorway next to a bicycle. A couple of African men, both looking bored and one of them chewing with his mouth open.

Her mouth framing a smile of fatuous relief, Alice slipped her shoes back on and pushed to her feet.

"You're not going anywhere." From behind her.

Alice swallowed in panic. At the far end of the platform, the lovebirds boarded the train, the woman leading the man by the hem of his t-shirt.

"I won't tell you again."

On board the train, the electronic beeping rang into the night outside. With that, the doors closed and the train pulled out of the station, leaving silence behind. In front of Alice, the opposite platform stood empty.

Kieran stepped forward into her field of vision, looking across the tracks as she did. "You're quite finished?"

Alice turned to face him, her eyes widening. Like the guests at the wedding, he too was dressed in formal wear, sans suit jacket. What appeared to be a flush of exertion was, on closer inspection, blood. Alice remembered the body tossed through the patio doors and closed her eyes against a tide of nausea.

Kieran stepped forward again, his brows lowered in contempt. "I'm sick of your stupidity. What I really should do now is just kill you where stand." His gaze on hers, he reached forward and took her hand in his own. Alice shuddered. Kieran's hand felt warm: hot, even, and slick with sweat. "Maybe I won't kill you just yet." He brought her hand to his lips and brushed his lips across the back of it. "I could just eat you." He tilted his hand and licked her thumb. "Just like old times," he murmured. "You never could get enough of that. Or," he said, sliding her sleeve up her arm from her wrist, "maybe I need a little more."

"Please," Alice breathed. "Please... don't do this."

"Ummm, no." Kieran's gaze grew hard. "You brought this on yourself—and ever since you dragged me through the courts on that bullshit lie, you never faced up to your mistake. So maybe I'll do this."

"I... I..."

Kieran leaned in closer, his nostrils flaring and his eyelids fluttering as if he were sexually aroused.

"Fear," he breathed. He licked his lips, swallowed and exhaled. "Right now, I need a little more than that."

Slowly Kieran sank into a crouch, his lips dragging down Alice's front to her stomach. "Food," he muttered, ripping open her dress and exposing her midriff. Resting his hands on her waist, Kieran pressed his nose and mouth into Alice's stomach.

"So good inside," he murmured, his breath misting against her skin. "So good."

His lips began to move wider apart.

Teeth now, scraping lightly back and forth to her navel as Kieran's head pushed into her again and again with more force. Alice's heart pounded like a jackhammer.

"I'm... I'm sorry."

Kieran's head slowed for a minute. Stopped. When he looked up, his expression was...*blank*. As blank as a brand new whiteboard. And for the first time in this nightmare, Alice could see the animal inside: something in the hooded gaze, the curl of the lip.

The showing of teeth.

"I'm sorry," she sobbed, raising a trembling hand to his scalp.

His head returned to her stomach, pushing into her with more force, the teeth scraping harder against the skin.

Alice brought her knee up into Kieran's jaw, making his teeth clack together. As he reeled, she swung one foot back and landed the toe of one stiletto in the flesh of his groin. Kieran collapsed on his side, doubled over.

Alice drew back and kicked him again, the sensation of flesh yielding against her shoe filling her with disgust. Kieran's hand shot out and grabbed her ankle mid-kick, pulling hard. Alice landed flat on her back, smacking her skull on the concrete. Pain flared from her scalp to her tailbone with the impact: eye-watering pain. She rolled onto her side, trying to right herself, blinking through a haze of tears. Kieran pushed to his hands and knees, his back arched like a bow.

Please, God, no.

The all-too-familiar chorus of groans amidst a staccato report of joints and bones shifting.

Alice stretched her legs out and with a cry of revulsion, shoved Kieran with both feet, sending him over the edge of the platform. Beyond the platform edge, a body thudded into a layer of stones. Alice rolled back onto her side and brought one hand up to the back of her head, fingertips gently probing beneath her hair. Her fingers discovered raw skin, and she yelped in response, bringing fresh tears of more than just pain. Battered and frightened, Alice wept.

Now came the harsh rending of fabric, from out of sight in the track bed.

Growls; low and menacing.

Alice sat up and reached into the inside pocket

of her jacket, pulling out one of the kitchen knives she had swiped from the Bingham Hotel kitchen on her dash into the night. She clutched the handle in her fist. On the other side of the tracks, a transparent trash bag, barely full, drifted back and forth in the night breeze. The same breeze blew past her, muffling her hearing and Alice grit her teeth in wretched annoyance. As quietly as she could, she slipped her shoes off and crept to the edge of the platform. Knife raised like a dagger, Alice swallowed and peered over the edge. Between the tracks below, tattered scraps of fabric lay on the rocks. Leather shoes lay torn wide open from the shoes' soles, like the petals of some grotesque flowers. Torn clothing lay nearby.

Alice scuttled back from the platform edge, hyperventilating now.

Goosebumps broke out across her skin.

Alice turned toward one end of the platform, seeing the same staircase leading to the ticket hall, and turned to the other end, seeing the slope of the platform into the track leading out the station. She looked over her shoulder, noting the shrubbery behind her. The worst thing to do now would be to look in one direction and not see the threat until it was too late.

Where the fuck...? she mouthed, her breathing shallow.

I'm not done with you by a long shot, Miss Morecambe, so you be sure to keep looking over your shoulder. Downwind,

Alice. That's where I'll be.

Images of licking a finger and then holding it up in the wind came to mind, and Alice chided herself mentally for it. Internal argument played back and forth: *it's stupid, why is it stupid, because it's a cliché, it might work, it might* not.

Alice gave a growl herself and licked one finger, holding it up in the air as a pattering sounded to her left. Wind, it seemed, blew from across the tracks in front of her, rustling the rubbish bag on the opposite platform. Alice frowned. But that didn't make any sense…

Pattering grew louder at her left side, and Alice pivoted toward it.

Glowing, reflective eyes in a mass of black fur bore down on her. Barrelling into Alice as she turned to run, the animal knocked her facedown and jolted the knife from her hand, where it clattered beside her on the platform. Alice flung out a hand for the knife, unwittingly grabbing the blade rather than the handle. Sharpened steel bit deep into her palm, raising a thin line of pain and blood. Alice spun to see the animal hunkered down, muzzle wrinkled back in a snarl, the sound so loud that Alice felt it vibrate through her and the ground.

Lunging forward, the animal clamped its jaws on Alice's thigh. Pain shot through as tremendous pressure on her leg increased. Blood welled from the wound on either side of the animal's jaws and Alice screamed, beating at the creature's snout with her fists—only to drive the knife blade deeper into her palm. Alice cried out with pain and slid her grip to the handle, not daring to let go of the knife completely. Blood slicked the handle, making the grip more tenuous. The animal worried further at her thigh, sinking its teeth in deeper. Something in Alice's leg ruptured and tore.

Alice cried in pain and drove the knife blade into the side of the creature's head over and over. Gashes opened beyond the ear with each blow.

…until one blow landed the blade deep in the ear itself.

The animal grunted. Stopped.

Alice's agony continued; a haze of pain.

She planted her hands on the animal's jaws, the muzzle slick and warm with blood. Working her fingers under the lips and the slick hardness of the teeth, she pulled until the jaws came apart, threads of saliva between the fangs and the bloodied limb. A fresh gout of blood ran anew.

Alice collapsed back onto the platform, her eyes wide and unfocused. The smell of blood and fur hung in the air. Miles overhead, the sky remained dark: starless and clear. Alice swallowed, suddenly feeling thirsty with her mouth rough like the bark of a tree. She tried to swallow again, her eyelids fluttering. Her breathing grew quick and shallow, her leg on fire, the rest of her skin cold as ice with the passage of moments.

Minutes.

More minutes.

Footsteps approached slowly at first, speeding up as they grew closer.

"Motherfucker," the man muttered, the young voice carrying a hint of a drawl. A slithering of fabric and a commotion beside her. Something thick and cool slid under her thigh and wrapped around it tight. Sudden pressure as the loop around her thigh drew tight like a hangman's noose.

A cool and firm hand rested on her stomach. "How we doing up there?" the man asked. "You hanging in there for me?"

Not finding the energy to lift her head, Alice peered down her cheek and sighted the balding head of her benefactor; his slender frame muscled into a blue t-shirt. Wasn't he cold? Alice slid a tongue across her lips, the motion rough on her tongue. Right now, she was cold.

So very, very cold.

EPILOGUE

Gwynne Holford Ward, Queen Mary's Hospital, London
14:50, 06/05/2016

Naomi seated herself in the chair beside the bed and looked around at the ward. Patients whiled away the time in a number of ways, from watching TV to napping. Naomi's gaze settled on one old man sitting by his bed, reading a Dan Brown paperback. Her gaze flitted back to the man's face as he sat wholly absorbed in his novel, before drifting over the man's form and settling on his feet, or rather, one slippered foot and one rounded stump. She wondered if he kept the slipper on so that he didn't have such a visual reminder of what was missing now.

Naomi turned her attention back to Alice, sitting on the edge of her bed. Looking leaner than before, the baggy Taz t-shirt from Looney Tunes hung off one shoulder. One leg ending in a bare foot with the nails unpainted, and one ending just before the knee in a bandaged stump. "Looks comfortable," she said.

Alice looked up with a slow deliberation, her brows low over listless eyes. "Oh, yeah. It's comfortable."

"Hey," Naomi said softly, leaning forward. "It won't be easy. I can only imagine how difficult it would be, but at least you made it this far. You're alive."

Alice inhaled and sighed. Her gaze drifted across the room. "Yeah. I'm alive."

"Don't you forget that." Naomi nodded, as if to underscore her words. "So when are they fitting the prosthetic?"

Alice breathed an open-mouth sigh. "Not for a while yet. They still need to make sure the swelling's gone down. They were looking at doing it today, but then, they don't want to take any chances."

"Of course not," Naomi said. "Smart move. But at least it will be done here?"

"Yeah."

"That's good. From what I know, you're in the care of London's best specialists to help you now, so hopefully that's one less thing to worry about."

"Yeah."

Naomi forced a smile. In the corridor off the ward, a pair of nurses walked past while poring over what appeared to be a tablet: one nurse holding the device close to the chest like a newborn infant, her companion peering over her shoulder in curiosity. Naomi gave a little smile at the notion that, once upon a time, a tablet was medication you swallowed rather than some cumbersome smartphone thing that was only really good for streaming TV and movies on. The only time she herself had been in hospital was when her appendix was taken out when she was a teenager. Back then, nurses referred to clipboards with handwritten notes.

Naomi turned her attention back to Alice. "Have you eaten yet?"

A slow shake of the head.

"How long until they feed you?"

A shrug of the shoulders.

Meanwhile, the Dan Brown reader continued to turn pages of his novel, as another patient shuffled in his bed and made himself comfortable. Silence continued to weigh on the ward, smothering like a blanket.

"Naomi," Alice said at last, "would you be offended if I asked you to leave? Right now, I really don't feel like talking. I appreciate you taking the—"

Naomi shook her head. "Honestly, it's okay. That's not a problem." She stood up and shoved a hand into her pocket, her keys jingling in response. "Just try not to spend too much time alone, okay? Let me know if you need anything."

Alice nodded and watched her go.

If she needed anything?

What she needed was her fucking leg back. Right now, she could still… feel her missing leg and her toes. The doctors gave their congenial smiles and assured her this was normal.

None of this was normal.

In the wake of Kieran's attack, Wayne was the first to arrive on the scene (as well as to ride to the hospital with her) and had the presence of mind to apply a tourniquet to stop Alice bleeding out. Although he had been drinking that night, the sight of Alice in a pool of her own blood sobered him up enough to help. With the help of another passenger and station staff, emergency services were alerted, and paramedics arrived at the station in short order, finding Alice unconscious. By the time paramedics rushed her into Accident and Emergency, the extent of damage and blood-loss made the decision clear. When Alice finally woke up, a bandage greeted her.

She cursed. Bawled. Screamed.

Folded to sedation by staff; and so the cycle of outbursts and sedation continued for a while. The outbursts themselves were draining: both physically and emotionally.

Time might heal all wounds, but wouldn't heal all of them completely. With the last of the tantrums behind her, Alice began to regain a sense of lucidity: enough that friends, loved ones and the emergency services felt they could finally ask that all-important question: *what happened?*

Alice told the truth. An animal had attacked her.

What kind of animal? Something like a dog or a wolf.

Something like? Yes. She had never seen either that large.

Yes, there were a few reports of a large dog or wolf involved in a number of recent incidents, but no, they didn't find one at the scene. Yes, the enquiries were ongoing.

Of course they were.

All of her inquisitors had reassured her as best possible that she was safe and that steps would be taken to find the animal before anyone else got hurt. Even her mother, who Alice suspected visited at persistent request from Becca, looked as though she genuinely worried about her wayward daughter. Alice glared in self-disgust. If they wanted to find the animal, all they had to do was keep an eye on Alice. *I'm not done with you by a long shot*, Kieran had said.

He wasn't kidding. According to Naomi, what was left of Richard was tossed in a goodie bag. The rest of his body could be anywhere. After that revelation (along with remorse and subsequent vomiting), Alice decided on solitude wherever possible.

Elbow on her knee, Alice rested her chin on her palm, gazing out the window. Those windows looked like they had security locks on them, and even if they opened fully, Gwynne Holford Ward was on the ground floor. To jump from that height, she'd be lucky to graze her knee, let alone break it or anything else. Even if she did, she might heal quickly.

Too quickly.

If hospital staff thought she was infected, they didn't look troubled by it.

Downwind, Alice. That's where I'll be.

Kieran was the least of her problems.

Alice ran a hand through her hair, clutching her scalp where a headache pulsed. They came more frequently now, over the last few days. Hospitals kept tight reins on medication, both the ones they dispensed as well as the ones that visitors might bring for the patients. Painkillers and sleeping pills were no different.

Staff, patients and visitors busied themselves as day wore into night. Hushed tones of staff and the occasional murmur or rustle of bedsheets if a patient stirred in sleep.

But not Alice.

Once again, sat on the edge of her bed.

This time with a Venus Razor in her hand.

You'll change.

She tightened her grip on the razor. Noted how the tendon moved beneath the skin.

You're going to change.

"Please…"

In her mind's eye, she stood naked, sobbing into a mirror as she tore at her hair. Agony shifting her bones and muscles with ruthless deliberation. Heat dizzying her, sweat slicking her skin. Nails turning to claws, drawing blood from her scalp. Sobs giving way to screams. Gums bleeding, split where the canines grew bigger, longer…

She gasped. Swallowed. Hyperventilating as she watched the darkness beyond the window.

What if there's a moon?

…matter. What if it doesn't matter?

Oh, no.

Alice turned her attention back to her wrists. Licked her lip.

…enough.

I'm not strong enough.

Please?

There would only be one chance to do it right: both cuts would need to be quick and deep. Savagely so.

Strong.

Please?

Alice trembled, lifting the razor. Tears leaked from her eyes.

Please let me be strong enough.

Please?

ABOUT THE AUTHOR

London native C.C. Adams is the author behind urban horror novella *But Worse Will Come*. His short fiction appears in publications such as Turn To Ash, Weirdbook Magazine and The Black Room Manuscripts. A member of the Horror Writers Association, he still lives in the capital. This is where he lifts weights, cooks—and looks for the perfect quote to set off the next dark delicacy. Look for him at www.ccadams.com.